The Splendor of Heaven

by

Saint Angilia

Heart-Glow Volume V

The Splendor of Heaven

by

Saint Angilia

Heart-Glow Volume V

SHEILAH R CRAFT

STARLIGHT BOOKS

STARLIGHT BOOKS

This novel is a work of fiction. Names, characters, places, and incidents either are products of the author's imagination or are used fictiously. Any resemblance to actual events, locales, or persons, living or dead, is entirely coincidental.

Cover and front piece photographs taken by Sheilah R Craft. The doll in the cover photograph represents Angilia as photographed in the Palace. The front piece photograph also depicts Angilia and her Uncle Patrick with Angel Bear that he gave her in the Angels Choir. Both versions of Angilia were customized by Laurie Lenz. The dolls were manufactured by the Tonner Doll Company. The author does not have any business affiliations with Tonner Doll Company or ANGELS Doll Studio.

ISBN-13: 978-0615965093

ISBN-10: 0615965091

AUTHOR'S NOTE

Writing this book, the fifth volume in my Heart-Glow series, has been a supreme honor and privilege. This volume is not the typical novel, as are the first four volumes and as will be the sixth volume. In this book, I literally become Angilia; I write the entire book from her experience and perspective. Knowing her—and the other characters—as intimately as I do means writing this book was never difficult or challenging.

Neither did the subject matter present any burdens. Writing about Heaven, God, Archangels Michael and Gabriel, and life after death allowed me to incorporate and to articulate my own beliefs; after all, Angilia and I share our Christian beliefs. Writing this book has been a blessing for me, in fact. My beliefs have strengthened. I find that I am becoming a better Christian and human being as a result of deeply connecting to my beliefs and knowledge about Heaven. I know that this pleases God the Father and Jesus the Savior—and Angilia as well.

Angilia, her family, and her friends have been alive and real to me since early 2012 when I had the several hours long waking dream that gifted me this novel series and these characters. I birthed these characters and their story, and they will forever remain ingrained in my soul and heart. They remain eternally alive for me. Dare I say that Angilia, Eric, Patrick, Matthew and the others are far more alive and real than many people I have met.

These characters' lives have purposes, and they live to fulfill those purposes. I, too, know my life's purpose, and I strive daily to accomplish my purpose. I know that writing these novels is a major element of my life's purpose. How can I know this? I have prayed to God about these novels, and feel assured I have His blessing to not only write them but to send them out into the world.

Part of the reason is that these characters, their experiences, and their story touch and affect people. Readers tell me that Angilia, Eric, Patrick, Matthew, and their family reinforce or renew their own faith, teach them significant life lessons, and fortify the importance of faith and family. I can never articulate how readers' responses humble and touch my soul. I wrote the first novel telling myself that if I reached even one person I would be content. I would know I had done what I am meant to do.

Four years after Heart-Glow: A Novel, volume one, was written and published, I feel even more strongly than ever that I was created to write these novels. I thank God for gifting me with the ability to do so.

--Sheilah R. Craft

December 2016

FOREWORD

This book truly is a miracle. More than thirteen years after my grandmother's physical death, I held and read her handwritten manuscript. The last time I had seen her familiar slanted cursive script was on the birthday card she gave me on the day she died, November 17, 2069.

May 8, 2083 was my graduation day from Oxford, and I was ever closer to my lifelong dream of opening Valdavia's first university. My grandmother remained the only person to whom I told this dream, and she continuously supported and encouraged me.

Early that morning, I went to University Church of St. Mary the Virgin to pray before the day grew chaotic. As I knelt, I felt a warm breeze surround me and a soft, gentle hand on my cheek. I opened my eyes. No one was there, of course. I knew that my grandmother had visited me.

This was confirmed at that moment when my great-granduncle Patrick manifested. He told me that Grandmother loves me, which I always knew (but was nice to hear), and that she had something for me. Uncle Patrick gave me a large envelope; inside were 82 parchment sheets—this manuscript. I read it right then and there, and felt such awe and wonder.

My grandmother had written about Heaven and life there—life after death. I was amazed by her words, her truth, but even more so when Uncle Patrick said that she wanted me to have and to publish this book. The proceeds would go toward my university. Uncle Patrick assured me that Archangel Michael approved of the book's publication.

I have read Grandmother's manuscript many times, and I can testify that my already firm Christian beliefs have only grown stronger, surer, and deeper. I possess no fear of death. My prayer is that everyone who reads this book lets go of any trepidation or fear of death they may feel. My grandmother presents the truest look at Heaven ever published, one from the perspective of someone who lived in Heaven prior to her birth and who now resides in Heaven since her death.

My grandmother's memoir, primarily about her existence in the Unborn Children Sphere and the Angels Choir preceding her physical birth, was published in 2020. That book stormed the world. So, too, will this book. But, if people are not supposed to remember their existence before birth, why does my grandmother? And why are her memories so detailed?

Simple. God uses my grandmother, Saint Angilia, to evangelize for Him. The miracles she has caused by praying for people, and now this book, prove God's existence, power, and love. I long knew of my grandmother's angelic past. I knew in many ways she belongs to the world. But to my brother Eric and me, she is Grandmother, the woman who loves us and who taught us about God.

I thank God for creating Angilia DeBruce Martineau Taylor.

--Patrick DeBruce Martineau Taylor

May 17, 2083

Valmondois, Valdavia

DEDICATED TO THE HOLY TRINITY:

GOD THE FATHER,

GOD THE SON,

GOD THE HOLY GHOST.

THANK YOU FOR CREATING ME, LOVING ME,

AND GIFTING ME THE APTITUDE TO WRITE THE

DeBRUCE MARTINEAU FAMILY'S STORY.

THIS SERIES AND ITS CHARACTERS

REMAIN BLESSINGS TO ME.

VERILY, VERILY, I SAY UNTO YOU, HE THAT HEARETH

MY WORD, AND BELIEVETH ON HIM THAT SENT ME,

HATH EVERLASTING LIFE, AND SHALL NOT COME

UNTO CONDEMNATION, BUT IS PASSED FROM

DEATH UNTO LIFE.

—JOHN 5:24

Heaven. The most beautiful, loving place in existence. The most mystical, paradisiacal place humans contemplate. No other place evokes as much thought or inspires as many questions as does Heaven. Why?

The simple answer: Heaven is unknown. Anything unknown breeds interest and curiosity. More importantly, though, Heaven remains beyond human understanding. Heaven is unlike any place humans have ever seen or experienced. Heaven is far grander, far more beautiful, and far more peaceful than anywhere on Earth. Heaven arouses the human brain; Heaven challenges people's concepts, ideas, and images. Because Heaven truly is the only perfect place to ever exist, it is beyond anyone's ability to accurately and completely conceptualize.

No matter how many times we read the biblical descriptions of Heaven, we can never truthfully imagine its splendor. No place on Earth has ever rivaled Heaven. Our imagination—our ability to form images—is restricted by our earthly experiences. Sure, there exist beautiful, peaceful places on Earth. I lived in one—Valdavia. Of course beauty and peace exist on Earth; God created Earth, after all, as the home for our physical beings. God's glory remains evident in all of His Creation. However, the beauty and peace we do know can never prepare us for the awesome wonders of Heaven.

Heaven remains impossible for the human mind to fathom, because Heaven really is unlike anyplace else known to humankind. For hundreds of centuries, Earth has witnessed multiple wars, destructions, and crimes—all caused by humans. Universal peace and love have been sporadic, never permanent. Poverty, hunger, illness, murder, addiction, abuse, abandonment—these are what people on Earth live with daily. When faced with all of this, how can anyone be expected to visualize Heaven in all of its loving glory?

Neither can we see Heaven, not even through the most powerful telescope. Heaven is not a planet or a star. Heaven is beyond anything the living can see, but that does not mean that Heaven is not real. On the contrary, Heaven is more real than the Earth, planets, and stars we do see and know. Furthermore, Heaven is eternal, and will remain long after the stars and galaxies cease to exist. 2 Peter 3:10 tells us that "*The heavens [the planets and the stars] will disappear with a roar.*" As terrifying as that prospect seems for many people, rest assured that after we enter Heaven, we will be with God. No living being can fully comprehend what that is truly like, for it is far grander than any earthly experience. On Earth, things often go wrong, but in Heaven, all is perfect—because God is perfect. No evil exists in Heaven. God's perfection, holiness, and love protect us.

Moreover, Heaven exists in a dimension completely unlike anything those living on Earth can ever know. Earth is the temporary home of our physical beings; Heaven is the eternal home of our spiritual beings. When believers' physical bodies die, their souls enter Heaven and are reborn in new bodies. They enter a new level of existence and consciousness.

No, God does not erase all memories related to our earthly lives. Far from it. We do remember the people and moments that are connected to pleasant memories. Because negativity and evil do not exist in Heaven, all of our painful and negative memories leave us the exact second we enter Heaven. We are left with happiness, love, peace, and beauty—for all eternity. How wondrous that feels!

Other aspects of our earthly lives fall away, as well. Our spiritual bodies never crave sleep. In fact, our spiritual bodies are whole and healthy; all physical ailments we may have suffered on Earth die with our physical bodies. We still look the same, yet no longer are we restricted by any physical limitations. All of the trials and tribulations of our earthly lives pass away into nothingness. We will never even remember them.

All of this is quite difficult for humans to understand. No memories of anyone or anything painful or bad. No more disease, illness, or physical pain. Our earthly lives are filled with pain— emotional and physical—to the extent that we cannot fathom life without pain. What would that even feel like?

Free. Eternal life without pain is the freest life we can know. My friend Arthur Brennan, my Uncle Patrick, and I readily testify to that. When I met Mr. Brennan on January 3, 2012, he was in a wheelchair, to which he had been confined for nearly five years at that point. Mr. Brennan had suffered an accident that damaged his legs. While that never damaged his spirit, it did hamper his ability to do all of the things he had previously enjoyed: hiking, gardening, taking his dog for walks, and driving.

Upon his death in 2016, though, Mr. Brennan regained his mobility. His charming house in Heaven has a flower garden that both Mr. and Mrs. Brennan enjoy tending. They also enjoy leisurely walks over the verdant hills and valleys of Heaven. Often, they are joined by their dog Taffy, which delights Mr. Brennan. (Yes, animals dwell in Heaven. More on that later.)

My Uncle Patrick was 19 when he died in a boating accident on July 19, 1977. He suffered internal damage and a broken spine. He did not die instantly, which means he felt the most excruciating pain. Had he survived, he would have been paralyzed from the neck down. I was Uncle Patrick's Spirit Guide, the one chosen to escort his spiritual body to Heaven. Patrick walked alongside me as we climbed the invisible staircase to Heaven. Patrick has remained incredibly active in the 106 years since his death. As an envoy angel, Patrick is often sent to Earth on God's behalf. Patrick's most visible role has been as a singer and songwriter, with the purpose of proving life after death.

Patrick was my Spirit Guide when I died in 2069. We once again climbed that invisible staircase to Heaven. The moment I arrived, I did something I had not been able to do since 2012. I ran. I ran to my parents. My right knee had been permanently damaged by a bullet in March 2012. I walked with a pronounced limp for the rest of my life. My heart was also damaged in the shooting, and, in fact, heart failure caused my death. Since my rebirth, however, those physical ailments no longer affect my body. I run, I walk, I dance, and I even ride my pony Starlight at a full gallop. I am completely free, as are my Uncle Patrick and Mr. Brennan—and every other person who resides in Heaven.

Not only are we reborn in flawless spiritual bodies, but we live in perpetual daylight. Heaven is one eternal, perfect day. Night never occurs in Heaven, for there is no need for night. Heaven is light and all that light connotes: clarity, truth, revelation, goodness, purity, security, warmth, and love. Constant light, a light unlike any ever seen on Earth, brighter and warmer than sunlight. Heaven's light is the most exquisite light—because Heaven's light emanates from God Himself. God's essence and love light Heaven with a golden glow more powerful than any electrical grid could ever hope to mimic. Words cannot describe this light, but if a comparison will help, I offer mine. Heaven's light is like being wrapped in the safe, warm, loving embrace of a beloved parent. Fear and loneliness become alien concepts, forgotten feelings, when we enter Heaven and are surrounded by its light.

Why is there no night in Heaven? As I mentioned earlier, Heaven exists in its own dimension, one unknown to all who dwell outside it. Planets do not exist in Heaven's dimension. Because Heaven has no sun and no moon, there can be no night. Perpetual daytime—light—is as impossible to imagine as is most every aspect of Heaven. After all, on Earth we are used to the darkness that occurs when the sun sinks below the horizon. One side of Earth is always bathed in shadow. Heaven is never cloaked in shadow— what we call night.

There is no need for night in Heaven. On Earth, night is typically when most people sleep, relaxing our minds and our bodies, often promoting healing and health. First of all, those of us in Heaven never tire or feel sleepy. We exist in perpetual consciousness, alertness, and activity. Secondly, as already mentioned, we remain eternally healthy. Therefore, we have no need of sleep's restorative benefits. Imagine never feeling tired or exhausted, never craving a comfortable bed on which to drift into sleep.

In fact, none of the homes in Heaven contain bedrooms, beds, or lamps. Yes, we have our own homes in Heaven, each perfect and filled with happiness. Each home is unique, created by God to suit its occupants. Jesus promises us that *"In my Father's house are many mansions. If it were not so, I would have told you. I go to prepare a place for you"* (John 14:2). For example, Mr. and Mrs.

Brennan live in a charming cottage, with a flower garden—complete with butterfly bushes. Ever since his infancy, Mr. Brennan enjoyed butterflies. In fact, his earliest memory is of trying to grab a butterfly in his mother's garden.

My in-laws, Mitchell and Katherine Taylor, have a lovely two-story home, where Katherine likewise has the flower garden she always wanted but never had the time to cultivate. Mitchell is content to sit on his rocking chair on the front porch, reading, visiting with family and friends, or engaging in a game of chess.

When Mitchell is not at home, he indulges in his favorite sport, golf. Since doctors aren't needed in Heaven, Mitchell has more time for golf. A golf course exists near his home. Mr. Brennan, my Uncle Eduardo, and many others join Mitchell. There is no competition as on Earth, though, only pure fun and enjoyment.

In fact, we all have the freedom to partake in what we enjoyed doing on Earth. Matthew draws and paints. I write books and music. Uncle Patrick plays sports. Katherine gardens. My father helps people.

Heaven is not all fun and games, though. We never slide into slothfulness. Everyone works, including God and Jesus. Jesus tells us so in John 5:17. "My Father worketh hitherto, and I work." We plant, cultivate, and harvest food for the heavenly feasts and celebrations. We tend to the animals and children. As our earthly work should, our heavenly work honors God.

My beloved parents' home is large, fittingly so. Many people frequently gather there. I rejoice every time I visit their home, for of course I cherish being with them, but I also truly enjoy talking with my ancestors—those whom I never had the chance to know. On Earth, genealogy remained a vitally important component of my life from early childhood. I maintained a huge family history book filled with facts, stories, and pictures of ancestors dating back to biblical times. When I lived on Earth, I knew I would meet my ancestors in Heaven, and I have. I longed for and looked forward to knowing them and talking with them. How wonderful to do so whenever I desire.

The first relative I met was my great-grandfather, Stefan DeBruce Martineau, when Archangel Michael brought me to the Third Sphere of the Angel Realm from the Unborn Children Sphere. Great-grandfather is a wise, kind man, and he taught me much in my time there. I did not know at the time that he was preparing me to become my uncle's Spirit Guide. Because of my role, Uncle Patrick was the second relative I knew.

Uncle Patrick's home is essentially a studio apartment—one large room. Patrick is rarely there, though, for he remains constantly active, mostly playing sports or singing when he isn't carrying out his duties as an envoy angel. When he is home, he either reads or writes, betraying the dunce image he cultivated in his teens. On Earth, Patrick hid his intelligence, introspection, and creativity as much as he could. Sensitive, poetry-writing teen boys faced teasing and bullying, and Patrick never wanted any of that to overshadow or interfere with his public role.

Since Patrick had been born a Prince de Valdavia, he performed frequent public duties and appointments. He enjoyed meeting people. More than that, he relished helping people, as well as encouraging or motivating them. While Patrick attended middle school, he became active in the Scout Guides, a national organization for children. His first official patronage was with the Athletic Association of Valdavia, which fostered and supported sports throughout the nation.

Patrick had been involved in spots most of his life, and while he was in high school he found his favorite sport—speed boat racing. He never intended that to be his career, though. His goal and desire was to become a career soldier in the Valdavian Army. Patrick had just begun that career and become a plebe when he died in the speed boat accident.

Now, Patrick frequently talks with athletes and soldiers, still pursuing his favorite subjects: physical fitness and international security. Patrick's primary goal as a soldier was to prevent war rather than to fight and kill people. He longed to promote and to educate every nation about peace. Patrick firmly believes that peace is attainable on Earth, and his earthly life would have been dedicated to that mission.

Like Uncle Patrick, Matthew and I do not stay at our home very often. We take walks or sit alongside a brook, talking, writing, and drawing. We visit family, friends, and welcome newcomers to Heaven. Sometimes we ride Starlight together; Matthew is no longer skittish of horses, as he was on Earth. When we are at our home, which is a delightful cottage reminiscent of the one in which Snow White found refuge, we do just as we did long ago in the Unborn Children Sphere. Matthew draws or paints, and I play the piano or write. Otherwise, we snuggle on the sofa, sometimes talking but often contently silent.

Words have long been unnecessary for Matthew and me to communicate. From the beginning of our friendship, we possessed an intuitive understanding of one another. Comfortable silence endures as one of our relationship's gifts. The love, support, and compassion we have shared for centuries allow us to dwell in tranquility, solidarity, and affection.

Matthew and I are kindred souls in every way; neither of us romantically loved another. Our union was predestined. My first consciousness is being in a beautiful, large, gold limestone temple, which I learned was the Unborn Children Sphere. The Unborn Children Sphere exists in the same dimension as Heaven and the Angel Realm. Peace dominates all of Heaven, and from the beginning of my existence, I felt the serenity and joy of that peace.

As I began walking, I saw these unborn souls doing whatever they were destined to perform on Earth. Orators practiced speeches at podiums. Scientists conducted experiments in laboratories. Astronomers studied Earth's planetary system through telescopes. Teachers conducted lessons in classrooms. Artists drew and painted. Musicians performed on various instruments peppered throughout the temple. Writers drafted manuscripts at desks. How marvelous, I thought, to have our lives' paths planned for us and to be able to hone our skills. I wondered what my destiny was as I wandered.

As I passed a massive bookshelf, I removed a book of poetry and began climbing a winding staircase. More unborn children greeted me as I ascended, and I smiled continuously. Everyone treated me with benevolence, and I instantly knew I was where I belonged—I was home. That feeling grew stronger once I entered the tower at the top of the staircase.

A piano and one boy were there, nothing and no one else. I walked closer to him, and he looked up and smiled at me. "You are new here. Welcome. I will be your friend."

"I would like that. My name is Angilia."

"Hello, Angilia. I am Matthew. Sit here beside me."

I did, and noticed a sketch book in his hand and colored pencils and paints on the floor. "You are an artist. May I see your work?" He showed me some drawings and watercolors of the Unborn Children Sphere and some of the unborn children. "These are beautiful, Matthew."

"Thank you. What book do you have?" I handed him the book, and he opened the pages and leafed through them. "Poetry. Would you mind reading some poems aloud while I draw? Please?"

I nodded, and read the first poem I opened to, *Epic of Gilgamesh*, the oldest written epic poem, composed in approximately 2100 B.C. I read several other poems, engrossed in the beauty of the words, images, similes, and ideas.

When I stopped, Matthew gently put his hand on my arm and looked at me with an expression I of course had never before seen. "You read poetry with such emotion and passion, Angilia. Even your face as you read reflected the emotions of the poems. I could not stop watching you as you read. Thank you for this experience."

I was speechless for a moment. Everything was new to me. "You are welcome, but I distracted you from your drawing."

"Not at all, Angilia. Because of you, I have drawn my most beautiful subject."

"Really? You drew an interpretation of one of the poems?"

"No." Matthew held his sketch book toward me. "You."

"Me? You drew me?" He smiled and nodded as I looked at my image. "I look like this? It feels odd to see myself."

"Yes, this is how you look, perfectly beautiful and angelic. I have met thousands of children here, Angilia, and I have never seen eyes that resemble yours, so intense, expressive, and that shade of blue."

"Really? So I am unlike the others here? Why?"

"Everyone here is unique, but most have similarities. Many children have blonde hair, as you do, but I have never seen that particular blonde before. Many have blue eyes, but not the same blue as yours. Your eyes are like the blue of a river or an ocean. You are unlike any other child here, yes, but I do not believe that is negative. After all, each of us was created by God, right?"

I smiled at Matthew. "Right. Matthew, I have never seen a river or an ocean. What do they look like?" I asked him. I learned something every minute.

Matthew stood and reached for my hand. "Come," he smiled, and led me down the staircase and into a room. An art gallery. As I glanced all around, Matthew guided me to a painting and suddenly stopped. "This is a beach with an ocean and mountains. See the blue of the water? Your eyes are that color, the color of the ocean."

"Oh," I gasped. I had only seen myself as he had drawn me with his colored pencils. He had made my eyes that color. "The ocean looks beautiful but very powerful. Did you paint this, Matthew?"

"No. One of the envoy angels did after a visit to Earth."

"Envoy angels? Earth? I feel so ignorant. I know nothing."

Matthew giggled. "You are not ignorant. None of us knew anything when we first arrived as baby souls, either. We all must learn, Angilia." Matthew explained envoy angels and Earth to me, and I began to understand.

"Will I ever meet an envoy angel?" I asked him.

"Perhaps. They sometimes come here to visit us."

I never met an envoy angel in the Unborn Children Sphere, but I sure did come to dearly love one—my Uncle Patrick!

Although I never met an envoy angel, I met others in the Unborn Children Sphere. You see, some souls remain there for what humans understand as hundreds of years before their earthly lives begin—before they are born to their parents.

While everyone I met is distinctive and memorable, some stand out in my memory, but not because I knew then the lives they would endure on Earth. Even prior to their physical births, these souls touched me deeply. My memories of these encounters remain vivid and detailed.

These encounters confirm that God creates every human being righteous. God creates each of us in His image, as Moses writes in Genesis 1:27: *"So God created man in his own image, in the image of God created he him; male and female he created them."* No, humans do not inherit God's flesh and bone; we cannot be physical children of God, because God is Spirit. However, Adam and Eve mirrored God. They were created in perfect health and gifted with immortality. Humankind was further provided reason and choice, which reflect God's intellect and freedom. Humans inherited God's likeness mentally, morally, and socially.

However, humans now also bear the imperfection of sin. Because God gives us choice—free will—we have the freedom to do as we please. We do not have to obey God, even though that is His wish for us. He intends our conscience to guide us into remaining *"very good"* (Genesis 1:31). Adam scarred the image of God within himself when he chose to disobey God. That scar has dwelt in every human since Adam.

All of us commit sin at some point in our earthly lives, but God promises redemption through our faith in Jesus Christ as His Son and our Savior (Ephesians 2:8-9). God understands that all humans stumble and fall, but He does not forsake anyone. Those who forsake Him, however, lose all hope of redemption and an eternal home in Heaven.

Once, Matthew was painting one of the rooms in the Unborn Children Sphere, one with curved walls, leveled floors, nooks, and—as do all rooms there—paneless windows. His easel stood in the center of the room, and he painted every feature of the room.

I stood watching him, and after a while, I sketched Matthew at work. As I watched him and drew, I noticed someone beside me. He looked from Matthew to me and smiled. "An artist drawing an artist. Two kindred souls. May I watch, too?"

"Of course. Matthew is an incredible artist."

The young man stood on his toes, leaned to the left, and studied Matthew's painting. "Yes. He is. His perspective, balance, and shadowing are expert. His depiction of this room is lifelike."

"You know art. Are you an artist?"

"Yes, I am. I paint or draw anything or anyone I see. I think I am good." He bowed his head, looked at me, and smiled. "That is vain, I suppose, and wrong here."

"God made us, and He gave us the abilities we have. We should use them. When we do, it honors Him. He should remain the focus. We would have nothing without Him," I replied.

"Yes, I suppose. But if He gave us a skill, are we not inherently exceptional at it?"

His question unsettled me. "Not necessarily. Our duty is to refine and polish that skill. God gifts us the ability to do something, but it is up to us to develop that and to become proficient at it. Not everyone does, so, no, not everyone is exceptionally talented."

"So if I desire to be the best, I need to draw and paint often? I need to practice. Is that right?"

"Yes. Matthew's work is so realistic because he draws and paints habitually. He has perfected his techniques. You should speak with Matthew. The two of you can work together sometimes."

"I would like that." He looked down at my sketchbook. "May I draw with you?"

"Of course you may."

"I would like to paint you. May I?" He paused. "What are you called?"

"Angilia. And, yes, you may, if you want."

He bowed. "I am indebted, Angilia."

I quickly studied my new friend. He was not tall, and he was rather pale. His dark brown hair was parted to one side and flat against his head. His eyes were blue, but a pale blue. How he stared through me. I had never seen an expression like his before, so penetrating and intense. I saw that many times in historic film footage and photographs during my earthly life. So have many of you, I'm sure.

Not long after our first meeting, Adolf and Matthew painted together for the first time. They asked me to accompany them, so I followed and sat in a window watching them. A cherub from the Angel Realm served as the subject of their painting.

Matthew and Adolf set up their easels next to one another, as they both wanted as close to the same perspective as possible. As the cherub played a flute, Matthew and Adolf sketched and then painted the cherub. When they both finished, the cherub waved and then winged its way back to the Angel Realm.

Each of them studied the other's painting, and each praised the other. Soon, others came by and commented that both paintings were true-to-life and expertly executed. Matthew smiled at Adolf, who blushed and appeared moved.

"Everyone is correct. Both of your paintings are well accomplished. In fact, they are almost identical except for your individual, unique brush strokes. Both of these will embellish the walls of the Sphere, and through them, both of your souls' imprints will remain here," I commented as I stood between Matthew and Adolf.

"I will like that, even if I never remember the Sphere," Adolf smiled.

"So will I," Matthew added.

"I still want to paint you, Angilia," Adolf reminded me.

Matthew suggested he do so right then since his easel and paints were prepared. So he did. I sat in the window again, and Matthew watched Adolf paint me. When he finished, Adolf stepped aside and asked Matthew, "Have I captured your fair maiden?"

Matthew stared at the painting. "Absolutely. May I keep this in the tower where I spend much of my time?"

"You may," Adolf bowed. "I hope I may visit you both there."

We assured Adolf he could, and Matthew carried the canvas to the tower. Once there, he leaned the painting against a wall and whispered, "I am glad we met Adolf."

"So am I, Matthew. Adolf should accomplish many honorable acts on Earth. I hope we somehow learn all he does accomplish. Chances are, we will not live on Earth at the same time as Adolf."

"I know." Matthew took my hand. "We are all meant to accomplish things. We all have a reason for our lives. We know that. Perhaps we will receive information about those we meet here, though we will not remember them once we are born."

"I know. But I can never anticipate forgetting you, Matthew."

"Nor I you."

Of course I never forgot Matthew—or anyone I met in the Unborn Children Sphere. When I was four and first saw a World War Two-era photograph of the Führer of Germany and Leader of the Nazi Party, I recognized him instantly. I asked my father if he knew anything about Adolf, and what I learned saddened me and hurt my heart. The kind, friendly Adolf I had known before our earthly lives became one of the cruelest, most amoral people. God is not responsible for Adolf's actions; Adolf chose the path he trod. He chose to forsake God. In fact, he claimed that he did not believe in God.

Adolf's story remains a perfect illustration of what it means to deny God and what that leads one toward. Another meeting Matthew and I had in the Sphere exemplifies the juxtaposition of Adolf's story. Once when Matthew and I walked down the winding staircase from our tower, I saw a young man sitting alone in a chair, bent over reading a book. I grabbed Matthew's hand and went to the man, and he looked up at us with his thin-lipped, kind smile. He greeted us and shook our hands. Matthew and I introduced ourselves. The man stood and bowed. He was quite tall, probably as tall as my Uncle Patrick, and he is six feet three inches tall. As he stood from his bow, he said, "I am pleased to meet you, Angilia and Matthew. I am Abraham."

His dark hair was mussed, and when he ran his hand through it a few times, I knew why. We talked to him for a while, and he read aloud from the book he held. I never forgot the stanza he read, and I looked it up once in my father's library. Abraham read to us the Epitaph of Thomas Gray's poem "Elegy Written in a Country Churchyard:"

Here rests his head upon the lap of Earth

A youth to Fortune and to Fame unknown.

Fair Science frown'd not on his humble birth,

And Melancholy mark'd him for her own.

Large was his bounty, and his soul sincere,

Heav'n did a recompense as largely send:

He gave to Mis'ry all he had, a tear,

He gain'd from Heav'n ('twas all he wish'd) a friend.

No farther seek his merits to disclose,

14

Or draw his frailties from their dread abode,

(There they alike in trembling hope repose)

The bosom of his Father and his God.

Abraham said something a moment later that I never forgot. He sat in the chair again, rested his arm on the back of the chair, and looked at the poem for a short while before he closed the book and left it on his lap. He took our hands in his, gave us a sad smile, and said, "I dare but hope people will think of me and remember me with the tenderness and truth of these lines. I can only pray that whatever I am meant to do on Earth will meet the trust and responsibility placed upon me, my dears."

I recollect feeling so incredibly despondent for the first time in my existence, and Matthew put his hand on my back, as he often did during our marriage, to soothe me. Abraham pulled me to him and held me while I cried. After a long while, he told me, "Angilia, please do not cry for me. Whatever my path through life, I will do what I must. I will live my destiny. So shall you." He kissed my cheek, pulled me away from his shoulder, and winked at me. "When you do think of me, know that no matter how difficult or full of despair my life, I did the best I could. You will go to Earth long after I return to Heaven, but we will meet again someday, my dear."

Abraham lived a life guided by the Bible and prayer. Yes, he was murdered for his beliefs and actions, but he died knowing he had lived the life intended for him. The entire world knows Abraham as the 16th President of the United States. He was correct, of course. We have reconnected in Heaven.

There is one more encounter in the Unborn Children Sphere which proves that God plans our lives long before we are created. I wrote about this meeting on November 17, 2001, my father's 47th birthday; I was five years old. Here is what I wrote, primarily for my father, although I also shared this with my husband Matthew when I became pregnant.

Daddy, someday you will read my diary about my life in the Unborn Children Sphere and the Angels Choir. You will know that I met a boy named Matthew in the Unborn Children Sphere, a boy who loves art and who was my best friend. I never forgot him. I never will. You know that Great-grandfather was my teacher in the Angels Choir and that he helped me learn about and prepare for my purpose there. You know that my purpose was to be Uncle Patrick's Spirit Guide, and I pray that the memory of that day no longer causes you pain. It shouldn't. Uncle Patrick is still around, Daddy, and someday you will see him, too. I know that. Seeing you the day I came to escort Uncle Patrick to Heaven remains the one most earth-shattering experience for me. I loved you at first sight, Daddy. I hope you know that.

I met someone else in the Unborn Children Sphere who changed my life before I saw you, though. I will never forget him. I never could. Someday I will see him again, I know that. So will you. I know that, too.

Once when I walked down the winding staircase from my and Matthew's tower, I instantly saw a man across the room. He saw me at the same moment. Our eyes locked. I felt odd, like I had to go to him, like I was compelled to walk across the room to him. He drew me to him as if he had lassoed and pulled me to him.

There is no age in the Unborn Children Sphere. Everyone takes on the physical manifestation of what they will look like on Earth, although everyone appears to be what we know as different ages. Some of the unborn children I met there appeared to be five years old, while others appeared to be in their 20s or 30s. It's different for everyone. I asked Michael about that once, when I was in the Angels Choir, and he told me that some people in the Unborn Children Sphere parallel the ages they will be on Earth during major events in their lives.

Maybe that is why I call the person I met a man, not a boy. He appeared to be in his 40s perhaps, like some of the diplomats who visit who are in that age range. That means something major will happen in his life during that time. I wonder what it will be. I honestly have no idea, although I wonder if we will witness that event, Daddy. It's within possibility.

I walked to the man and felt so startled when I looked at him and into his eyes. His eyes amazed me. His eyes looked like my eyes. No one else I met in the Unborn Children Sphere had eyes that resembled mine. There were quite a lot of people there with blue eyes, but no one else with turquoise eyes. I never saw anyone else with these eyes until I came for Uncle Patrick and saw you, Daddy. I have your eyes. So does the man I met in the Unborn Children Sphere.

He smiled at me, and I felt strange. I can now describe how I felt. My heart fluttered. It did so again when he pulled me into a hug and held me tight for a long while. Something about him seemed so familiar, warm, and honest. I loved him at that moment. That seems odd, I know, since I had just seen him for the first time and not spoken with him yet. I loved him instantly. I don't know how else to explain how I felt, and I hope that makes sense.

He finally spoke, as he still held me to him. He was much taller than I was, but he held me close to him and said, 'I love you so very much. I never thought I would see you until my birth. You are all I imagined you to be'.

I looked up at him, and I am sure my face betrayed my confusion. He took my hand and led me to a settee away from everyone else, where we could talk alone. He smiled and held my hands. 'You do not know who I am, do you, Angilia?' He knew my name, and my heart fluttered again when he said my name. I felt as though I recognized him, even though I had never seen him before. I knew I loved him.

'I'm not sure. I feel as if we have known each other forever, and yet I have never seen you before. I do love you, I know that.'

He smiled at me and pulled me close to him again. 'I love you, too, so very much. We will know each other for all time. We met here, but we will meet again on Earth in the future. You and I are meant to be together, part of the same soul.' He looked into my eyes, and suddenly I knew. I knew who he is, who he will always be.

He nodded as he looked deep into my eyes, into my soul's depth. I placed my hand over his cheek, and it was as if an electric shock went through my whole being. 'I do know you.' I whispered. 'You are my son, my only child.'

'Yes. You are my mother. I am your son. You know me. I know you. You are my mother Angilia. I am your son Eric. You love me. I love you. That is how it is and will be for all eternity. We are meant to be mother and son. God placed us together, and thus it will always be. I love you. Carry that with you while you await my arrival.'

I nodded, and we hugged. He kissed my cheek. We sat together for what seemed like a long time. I never saw him again, for it seemed not long after that meeting with Eric that Michael came to take me to the Angels Choir. I somehow feel I will give birth to him in my mid-20s.

I never forgot Eric. How could I? I never told anyone about him, though. This is the first I have mentioned him at all.

Our births and deaths are established by God when He creates us. Only He determines the dates and times of our births and deaths. He may not always control the circumstances of our deaths, though, because God has no dominion over those who choose to commit violent or careless acts that cause people's deaths. My Uncle Patrick is a prime example of God's plan. Patrick was born on January 6, 1958, and he died on July 19, 1977. He was 19 years old. Patrick's lifespan had been decided when God created his soul.

God always meant for Patrick to die on July 19, 1977, but God did not cause the speed boat accident that killed Patrick. Had Patrick not gone speed boating that day, he would have died in another manner. Why would God want someone to die at only 19? God had a much grander purpose for Patrick, one that Patrick has lived since his physical death. Patrick has served God as an envoy angel, spreading the truth of eternal life. Everything Patrick has done—the recordings, public appearances, interviews—is with God's blessing and to serve God.

Each of us has a purpose, a reason for being created—the reason we exist. God has a plan for our lives. Our duty is to open ourselves up to that purpose and to fulfill that during our earthly lives. Not everyone does that, of course; some people forge their own paths in life.

Our purpose is not directly tied to our job titles, educations, deeds, or relationships. These should all play roles in fulfilling our purpose, however. God's will for each of His children is that we follow His heart, allowing Him to fill us and work through us every moment of our lives on Earth. He desires us to develop an intimate relationship with His Son, Jesus. He wants us to commit to Jesus, for in doing so, we commit to our lifelong mission. Luke wrote Jesus' words in Acts 1:8. *"But ye shall receive power, after that the Holy Ghost is come upon you: and ye shall be witness unto me both in Jerusalem, and in all Judea, and in Samaria, and unto the uttermost part of the earth."* We are called to witness for Jesus.

If we allow the story of our lives to unfold as we connect with Jesus—the Word—we live the life intended for us. Everything we do aligns with that. In fact, the why of our existence begins with the heart, as stated by Solomon in Proverbs 4:24. *"Keep thy heart with all diligence; for out of it are the issues of life."* We must guard our hearts, and our minds, for these (emotion and logic) guide everything we do.

God furthermore desires three things of us. One is that His followers are faithful to Him. Another is that parents nurture their children in righteousness. Lastly, He desires that His Word—the Truth—spread to every nation. Samuel wrote, *"And I will raise me up a faithful priest, that shall do according to that which is in mine heart and in my mind: and I will build him a sure house; and he shall walk before mine anointed for ever"* (1 Samuel 2:35). Do what is in God's heart and mind; align your heart and mind with God's. God's true purpose for each of us is to live for Him and to honor Him in all we do.

How each of us does so is not important necessarily. People do so through art, literature, serving food, music, teaching, sweeping floors, and sundry other occupations. We can honor God no matter our jobs. He has no regard for titles and awards. His concern is how we live for Him and serve Him in all we do.

Anytime someone asked me about the meaning of life, I thought of Paul Gauguin's 1897 painting. Gauguin wrote three questions in the upper left corner:

D'où Venons Nous

Que Sommes Nous

Où Allons Nous

The first question, Where do we come from?, is easy to answer. We all come from God. He creates every living being.

Question two relates to the first question. What are we? We are souls. We begin existence as souls in the Unborn Children Sphere. When we are born, our souls inhabit physical bodies, which are temporary homes for our souls. Upon our deaths, the physical bodies are no longer needed. Our souls exist for all eternity.

Where are we going? Gauguin's third question has two possible answers: Heaven or Hell. Those whose faith and belief in God remain firmly implanted throughout their earthly lives, those who live according to God's laws, spend eternity in Heaven with God. Those who reject the Holy Ghost spend eternity in Hell with Lucifer.

Lucifer remains the prime example of one who begins as a child of God, imbued with His love. Lucifer was the second most beautiful being in Heaven; God is the most beautiful. Lucifer sat at God's right hand, a place of honor. He was loved. He was trusted. Even his name indicates God's feelings for him—it means 'Light Bearer.' Lucifer was magnificent. Lucifer was an archangel, along with Michael.

However, even angels are endowed with free will. Lucifer became unsatisfied with the honors and blessings bestowed upon him. Sitting beside God and being the second most beautiful being in Heaven were not enough for him. Lucifer became jealous of God. He desired God's dominion. He wanted to rule Heaven, to usurp God. We all know that a battle ensued. Lucifer convinced other angels to follow him, and they became his unholy army. Michael and his army of angels outnumbered and overpowered Lucifer.

As a result, God granted Lucifer dominion over a kingdom—Hell. Lucifer reigns, and his legion of fallen angels serve him. Hell is truly dark, fiery, and full of unimaginable torment. We read one example of this in Luke 16:22-26: *"And it came to pass, that the beggar died, and was carried by the angels into Abraham's bosom: the rich man also died, and was buried; And in hell he lift up his eyes, being in torments, and seeth Abraham afar off, and Lazarus in his bosom. And he cried and said, Father Abraham, have mercy on me, and send Lazarus, that he may dip the tip of his finger in water, and cool my tongue; for I am tormented in this flame. But Abraham said, Son, remember that thou in thy lifetime receivedst thy good things, and likewise Lazarus evil things: but now he is comforted, and thou art tormented. And beside all this, between us and you there is a great gulf fixed: so that they which would pass from hence to you cannot; neither can they pass to us, that would come from thence."* This passage proves that those in Hell can see Heaven and its glories. What greater anguish than to see the love, peace, and beauty of Heaven while suffering amidst the intense flames of Hell?

But where is Hell? Do we know? Yes. God tells us in Matthew 12:40 that *"For as Jonas was three days and three nights in the whale's belly; so shall the Son of man be three days and three nights in the heart of the earth."* Hell is at the center of the Earth. Hell is a place of separation and punishment.

Yes, Jesus spent the time between His Crucifixion and His Resurrection in Hell. Why? Jesus' death paid the price for our sins; His blood remains our salvation. After He died on the cross, Jesus went to Hell to prove His triumph over death and sin, as stated in Colossians 2:15: *"And having spoiled principalities and powers, he made a show of them openly, triumphing over them in it."* Before He departed Hell, Jesus took *"the keys of hell and death"* from Lucifer, the devil (Revelation 1:18). This act further solidifies the truth that those who are saved by Jesus' blood can never truly die and are protected from Hell.

That does not mean we are never tempted or persecuted by Lucifer. We are, for he is relentless in his determination to claim as many souls as possible. Lucifer will say or do anything in order to seduce people away from God. He tried to tempt Jesus, as told to us in Matthew 4:1-11.

Just as he came to Jesus, Lucifer visited me once. On July 13, 2013, I was working in the basement recording studio. I had just finished recording a demo of a new song, and the studio became extremely cold. I knew instantly that Uncle Patrick wasn't visiting, because angel manifestations generate warmth. Coldness indicates evil spirits. Whose, though?

Before I had a chance to think further, strong, cold hands grabbed my shoulders. I knew immediately, for only one being could be that chillingly cold. "Lucifer," I stated. "Why are you here? You know that you are not welcome here."

"And why is that? I once sat on God's right hand."

I turned to face him. "Once, yes. Past tense. You chose to end that, to forsake your seat of honor. You had beauty, wisdom, talent, and perfection, yet you wanted more. You wanted to be worshipped like God. Your greed and ego brought you down. You turned against God, who had created you in love and who had gifted you and honored you above all others."

"Whose ego is greater? God refuses to share His glory, His power, His dominion. He is greedy, seeking to be worshipped more than anyone else."

"He is the sole Creator. He gives life to everyone and everything. He asks for our faith, loyalty, and worship in return for the gifts he bestows upon us," I countered calmly yet assertively.

Lucifer laughed, a deep guttural sound I have never again heard. "Gifts? He let you nearly be killed by an assassin's bullet, and yet you defend Him."

"No. God had nothing to do with the shooting. Gregor Jamieson had, like you, turned his back on God; he chose to follow you instead. You are responsible for Jamieson's actions. You. Why? Because my father and I believe in and worship God?" I saw a smile form on his black lips. "My father and I are not afraid of death. As children of God who obey Him, we are both confident that we will be welcomed into Heaven when our earthly lives end. Even if I had died last year, I would be with God in Heaven, not with you in Hell."

"How can you be sure, Angilia, angel girl?"

"Because God and His Son Jesus tell me so." I looked at Lucifer, once so very beautiful and now so unutterably vile. "God made us and He named us. Your name Lucifer means 'Light Bearer.' You were the son of the morning. Now you are pure darkness. And for what? To reign over Hell for all eternity? Those who follow you and dwell in Hell no longer praise you once they are there, do they? They curse you for luring them to eternal torture. How proud you must feel."

"Do not mock me! How would you know what Hell is like?"

"Hell is the antithesis of Heaven."

"Hell is my domain, my kingdom. Come, you will have an honor no living soul has been granted. You, Angilia, will visit Hell and see my kingdom for yourself."

Lucifer pulled me to him, held me tight, and departed through the floor and palace foundation. Alice's spiral down the rabbit hole could never be as surreal as my journey with Lucifer. In mere seconds, he sped through the ground to the center of Earth— to Hell. Heat assaulted me immediately. The only refuge from the total darkness was the light from the fires. It took several moments for my eyes to adjust.

My senses were also assaulted. I felt the heat. I smelled burning flesh. I saw dead souls writhing in agony and attempting to escape the fiery pits. I heard the moans, screams, and pleas of thousands of souls, some of whom begged God to save them. My heart ached. They had denied God during their earthly lives, but they sought His comfort once confronted with the reality of their eternal damnation.

Lucifer seemed to sense my thoughts. He took me to the precipice of the pit and forced me to look closely. Several poor souls reached for Lucifer and begged him to release them from the pit. He laughed that disturbing cackle in response.

One man reached up at me, and he actually cried. "You are not one of us. Did you come to save us? Please save me."

I shook my head. "No. I cannot save any of you. You brought yourselves here." He asked how. "You denied God as your Creator and His Son Jesus as your Savior. This is your sentence. There is nothing I can do but pray for your master."

"Pray for me?" Lucifer asked through clenched teeth. "Why? God can do nothing for me any longer."

"Yes, He can, Lucifer. You loved God once. He still loves you. If you could put away your pride and earnestly ask His forgiveness, He will grant it." He looked into my eyes, silent but attentive.

"You were the most beautiful angel He created. Even Michael says so. Michael told me about you, about you as the Chief Covering angel who was very close to God. You were cloaked in gold and jewels. Somewhere deep in your soul that Lucifer still exists. He can reclaim you. Let him. Let go of your pride and anger."

As I spoke, I saw something hopeful glimmer in his dark eyes: longing. Then he slightly recoiled, and it disappeared. He once more appeared haughty. "How dare you presume to know me? What makes you think I would ask for God's forgiveness?"

I looked into his eyes. "So that you can reclaim what you once were and had: a beloved, trusted archangel seated alongside God in His throne room."

That longing briefly flitted through him, but he once more denied it. "His throne room, not mine. Why would I want to be second to anyone, when here I have my own throne?"

"Why would you not? Why spend eternity in this dark, burning abyss of torture? Why not return to light, love, and peace?"

"Why allow my Creator to force me into subservience? Why was I not given power and dominion? Why would I be God's lapdog, when I can rule over my own kingdom?"

"Are you happy here?"

"Happy? I do not need happiness. I have what I want here."

"I'm sorry," I said. Lucifer raged, and he shoved me. A hand from the fiery pit grabbed my leg, and I looked down—and gasped. "Gregor Jamieson." I had last seen him more than one year earlier, the day he committed suicide.

"I can still have my revenge. Let me torture her to death," he begged Lucifer.

"You cannot hurt me any longer. You have no power over me, Gregor Jamieson. Neither you nor the fires of Hell can harm me. I belong to God, and He protects me."

Jamieson smirked and pulled me into the pit. The whole of Hell trembled, as if shaken by an earthquake. God's wrath.

"Let her go!" Lucifer commanded. "Now!"

Jamieson did let go of me, but he did not lift me out of the pit. I struggled to climb out, and I felt many hands on me as the condemned grabbed me. Were they trying to hold me in the pit? Were they trying to leave with me? I will never know. As Hell rattled again, Lucifer betrayed fear. He reached down and lifted me from the pit.

"Do not forget my kingdom, Angilia."

"I won't. I will tell people how wretched and deplorable Hell is."

Lucifer appeared offended. Had he really expected me to find Hell appealing and welcoming? How could I do that? Hell truly is the opposite of Heaven.

Without another word, Lucifer took me home, back to the recording studio. As he turned to leave, I put my hand on his arm and said, "I will pray for you, Lucifer." He never looked at me, but he nodded once.

Yes, Lucifer did feel regret for his rebellion, but his pride kept him from asking God for forgiveness. Lucifer had to want a return to his former seat of honor in Heaven. I would pray that he open his heart to God once again.

I continue to pray for Lucifer, but thus far he has remained steadfast in his separation from God. I have never seen him since that day, yet I pray that I do—not the Lucifer the world knows as Satan, but the Lucifer who was the shining archangel.

Other angels from the Archangel Choir whom I met while in the Unborn Children Sphere and the Angel Realm include Gabriel and Michael. Gabriel is God's supreme divine messenger or envoy angel, and he was sent by God to Zacharias and Mary. Gabriel has a special affinity to parents and children, creators, and the arts.

Gabriel is the angel above all other angels who was sent to Zacharias to inform him that his infertile wife Elizabeth would give birth to a very special boy named John. Luke 1:3 tells us that Elizabeth was barren, but God opened her womb for John, who would precede his cousin.

John's cousin's mother received a divine visit from Gabriel six months later. Mary, a relative of Elizabeth, was young, unmarried, and dwelt in Nazareth. She never questioned or doubted Gabriel when he told her that she would give birth to God's Son, Jesus, as related in Luke 1:26-27.

Gabriel was chosen by God to deliver these most important of messages to Zacharias and Mary. We know Elizabeth's son as John the Baptist, the young man who baptized his cousin Jesus. Gabriel was entrusted with another major task. He sent the book of Revelation to the Apostle John, as stated in Revelation 1:1-2.

Gabriel, like all of God's supreme angels, is remarkably beautiful, fair and golden-haired. Gabriel is my musical partner, beginning in the Angels Choir and now in Heaven. We play piano duets, often accompanied by angels playing violins, harps, and horns.

Another favorite task of Gabriel's comes as no surprise to those who know him, and it charms us all. Gabriel is the big brother figure to all youngsters who dwell in Heaven. Babies, toddlers, and children all receive Gabriel's attention and extra love. Not only does he play with them, but Gabriel reads to them, tells them stories, and teaches them about the wondrous home they now have. Few things warm my soul as does witnessing Gabriel with the young souls in Heaven.

Those youngsters are never sad, scared, or lonely. They remain content, safe, and loved. I see these precious young souls, and they are each beautiful, joyous, and full of laughter. Although their parents and loved ones grieve them, these young ones are free from any suffering or angst. I wish grieving parents could see their children in Heaven, so carefree, laughing, playing, learning, living eternally. If they could see their children just once, their immense grief would subside. Of course they will miss their beloved babies for the rest of their earthly lives, but they would no longer deeply mourn. They couldn't. Seeing Heaven's children fills me with joy and peace.

So does Archangel Michael, the leader of all angels and of God's army. As such, Michael is the one who combats Lucifer, or Satan as he is called as the ruler of Hell. Michael defeated Lucifer when Lucifer rebelled and rallied one-third of the angels to follow him. Lucifer and his fellow fallen angels were banished to Hell, where they remain.

Michael is a grand, gorgeous soldier of God, and he is a champion of all Christians. Michael escorts the newly deceased to their heavenly judgment. How he rejoices for every soul welcomed into Heaven! Michael's greatest desire is for everyone to live eternally in Heaven. But for those who do not, Michael weeps. He, too, knows the torments of Hell, and he does not wish that for anyone. Every time a soul is banished to Hell, Michael grieves. He cannot fathom why anyone would willingly forsake God and Heaven to spend eternity tortured in the fires of Hell. Neither can I.

Michael is the most beautiful angel I have ever seen. His beauty is an outward expression of the godliness, purity, and beauty of his being, his soul. Angels can never be what humans define as unattractive, for angels are filled with God and reflect His perfection.

Michael never backs away from a battle with Lucifer (Satan). Michael guarded Moses' tomb from Satan, as described in Jude 1:19: *"Yet Michael, the archangel, when contending with the devil he disputed about the body of Moses, durst not bring against him a railing accusation, but said, The Lord rebuke thee."* Michael will always defeat Satan, the former archangel Lucifer. Their final battle is foretold in Revelation 12:7-17.

Eventually, Satan will be put in the bottomless pit for 1,000 years, during which he shall not be allowed to tempt anyone (Revelation 20:1-3). At the end of the 1,000 years, Satan will be released from the pit, and he will resume his evil ways. He will gather the wicked to fight against God and His people. But God will bring down fire from Heaven to destroy the wicked. Satan will then be cast into the lake of fire to suffer eternal torment. Satan will never again tempt anyone; his reign of power will end (Revelation 20:7-10). This is reiterated in the Old Testament, in Nahum 1:9.

Lucifer knows his fate. He knows what awaits him. He understands the repercussions of his sin, yet he steadfastly refuses to let go of his pride and ask for God's forgiveness. How utterly sad this makes me. How could one who had been the preeminent angel in Heaven choose to spend eternity in Hell? Pride is a deadly sin for this very reason. *"Pride goeth before destruction, and an haughty spirit before a fall,"* wrote Solomon in Proverbs 16:18.

Sin can never prosper nor profit on Earth. Humans are not perfect as were Adam and Eve prior to their fall. We each sin, some more than others. Many people do repent and ask for God's forgiveness. That is what He wants us to do. God does not want His children to forge a dysfunctional relationship with Him.

God is our Heavenly Father, and comparable to our earthly fathers, He loves us, wants the best for us, teaches us, and wishes us to obey Him. If we choose to disregard or to disobey Him, He will reprimand us—just as our earthly fathers should. When either of our fathers rebuke us, that is for our benefit. They do so because they do love us and wish the best for us, not because they do not care. If they truly did not care, they would do nothing and continue to let us commit wrong.

But neither of our fathers do that. They care too much. God does not want the separation between us to become permanent. He created us so that we would live with Him in Heaven for all time. Originally, the intention was that humans would live our earthly lives as stewards of the Earth, its animals, and its plants. We would work, sustain ourselves, love one another and God, and obey God.

Lucifer changed that by tempting Eve, who in turn tempted Adam. Both knowingly and willingly disobeyed God. That brought sin into the equation, and thus, through free will, opened the door for humans to choose sin.

Of course, God never wants us to choose sin, but He realizes that no human being attains perfection. He accepts that all humans sin. Even one of God's chosen—Moses—sinned by not *"sanctify[ing] God in the eyes of the people"* (Numbers 20:12). Moses was punished for that sin, prohibited from entering the Promised Land of Israel. Moses' anger is an example of an all-too-common human response, but Numbers 20 proves how such reactions displease God.

John the Evangelist provides the antidote we need for sin. In 1 John 1:9, John tells us that *"If we confess our sins he is faithful and just to forgive our sins and cleanse us from all unrighteousness."* Simply put, to confess in this context means to agree with God; in other words, we need to see our sins as God sees them.

The Apostle Paul echoes this message in 2 Corinthians 7:10, telling us that *"Godly sorrow brings repentance that leads to salvation and leaves no regret, but worldly sorrow brings death."* What is worldly sorrow? This is the feeling some people have when they are caught doing wrong. They are not sorry for the wrong-doing, but rather for getting caught. There is no yearning to change their behavior, to stop the wrong-doing. There is only the wish to not get caught again.

Godly sorrow means we see our sins as Jesus sees us committing them. We see how our sins break His heart. We see our sins from Christ's perspective. The truth that my sins deeply wounded God my Father and Jesus my Savior did more than any other biblical lesson to lead me toward repentance. How could I deliberately hurt my Heavenly Father and my Savior? Why would I want to?

Not everyone feels this way, of course. While I lived on Earth, I heard many people claim that it was acceptable to sin, because they have impunity. How tragic and deluded. Grace does not mean people can sin without consequences. Far from that. In Ephesians 4:30, Apostle Paul clearly instructs us *"And do not grieve the Holy Spirit of God, with whom you were sealed for the day of redemption."* Do not aggrieve God, but rather seek to please Him, for you were branded as His own for the final deliverance from sin.

When I worked with the King Philippe High School chapter of Christ on Campus, one young man asked me a serious and thought-provoking question. "What if a Christian dies before he can repent of a sin? Would he still go to Heaven, or would he be condemned to Hell?" The students and I held a gloriously enlightening discussion and Bible study that afternoon. I began by assuring them that a Christian can die in sin and die without asking for forgiveness and go to Heaven—with one condition. That person must truly be saved. How can one know? We are saved by trusting Jesus Christ. Apostle Paul informs us so in Philippians 3:8-9.

Jesus paid for—He bought—our salvation with His blood, as Apostle Paul says in Romans 4:4-5: *"Now to him that worketh is the reward not reckoned of grace, but of debt. But to him that worketh not, but believeth on him that justifieth the ungodly, his faith is counted for righteousness."* Jesus Christ is our ticket to Heaven. All we need to do is trust Jesus Christ; trusting Him completely is the only way, not our actions or deeds. In order to gain an eternal home in Heaven, we must trust Jesus Christ.

What does it mean to trust Jesus? First, acknowledge that we cannot get ourselves into Heaven, not by our good deeds. We need to ask Jesus' forgiveness of our sins, and realize that He died for our sins. Afterward, a new life begins as a follower of Christ. As such, we rely upon Jesus for all aspects of our lives, not just for forgiveness of sin. Jesus becomes our primary teacher. We learn from Him. We learn how to live lives that are according to His will and His truth. We let Him guide us through our earthly lives. Doing so brings the utmost peace, joy, hope, and inner truth that one can ever experience. Trusting Jesus is truly life-changing.

Our true beliefs determine how we live. To trust Jesus expressly means that we believe, without question or doubt, what He tells us. If we do believe His statements are true, our lives will reflect that belief.

Those who say they trust Him, yet continue living the lives they crave, do not really trust Jesus. John the Evangelist and the Apostle Paul address this, John in 1 John 1:6-2:2, and Paul in Romans 6:1-2. *"What shall we say then? Shall we continue in sin, that grace may abound? God forbid. How shall we, that are dead to sin, live any longer therein?*" Why would we desire to become ensnared in sin once more? What is the gain in sin?

"But what about Adam and Eve? They sinned, and God punished them. Are they in Heaven?" another COC member asked. We examined the biblical evidence. After more than two hours of discussion, questions, and prayer for guidance, we had the answer. (Yes, I could have told them the answer, but I needed them to see the Truth.)

Yes, Adam and Eve disobeyed God and sinned against Him. However, they never lost their belief and trust in God. How do we know this? All the Bible reveals is that Eve gave birth to three sons after she and Adam were banished from Eden. By analyzing their son Abel, we get our answer.

Abel and his older brother Cain presented offerings to God. Abel's offering was by faith, as written in the New Testament Hebrews 11:4. To clarify, Cain's offering was not driven by his faith, but by his own yearning. Abel offered God the "*more excellent sacrifice,*" the best he possessed. Cain did not give God his best. Abel offered with a heart that believed in God and through faith, whereas Cain kept his best for himself.

From where did Abel learn of God? From his parents, Adam and Eve, of course. Until Seth, the third son, was born, four humans existed on Earth: Adam, Eve, Cain, and Abel. Cain and Abel could never have learned about God elsewhere. Yes, Abel's faith was strong, while his brother's was weak, but both young men were taught the same. Remember, God infused Adam and Eve (and all descendants) with free will, and Cain chose what and how to believe.

Even after their expulsion from Eden, Adam and Eve knew God and taught their sons about Him. God never forsook them, either. In fact, God made clear, in the encounter with Adam, Eve, and the serpent, in the Garden of Eden, that Adam's and Eve's descendant would ultimately crush the serpent (Lucifer/Satan). As God told them, "*I will put enmity between thy seed and her seed; it shall bruise thy head, and thou shalt bruise his heel*" (Genesis 3:15).

Eve's seed would crush Satan. Who is this seed? Through Seth, in a genealogy containing the great prophets, Noah, Abraham, David, and Solomon, we get to Joseph, who wed Mary of Nazareth. Joseph was the man chosen by God to be the earthly father of the Savior, Jesus Christ (as provided in Matthew).

The genealogy to Mary of Nazareth is the same through David. However, David's son Nathan leads to Mary, and of course her son Jesus (traced in Luke).

Even though Adam and Eve sinned, they obviously asked God's forgiveness. They maintained their faith in God, which they taught to their two sons, even though Cain's faith was weak. Abel, however, proved his faith through his life and his actions. Because Adam and Eve believed and had faith, God made them the beginning of Jesus' earthly genealogy. God loves them. Therefore, Adam and Eve live in Heaven.

Another serious question a COC member asked me after a classmate's suicide is, "Can a Christian who commits suicide go to Heaven?" Of course suicide is wrong. Depression, the most common cause of suicide, is an understandably critical disorder that affects how one thinks, feels, and acts. Like with all disorders, the symptoms are not the choice of those who suffer. No one chooses this, and God understands that.

While I do comprehend how difficult depression, bullying, abuse, or any traumatic situation is, I want to remind everyone that a believer can always turn to God for peace and strength. God is stronger than any of us are, and He alone knows how everything will turn out at the end of the struggle. Even when we can't see the light and the hope, God can. He will always be there, through every trauma.

We all suffer during our earthly lives. God sometimes brings us to the point of utter despair and exasperation for a reason. He wants us to stop trying to live our earthly lives on our strength and will alone. He wants us instead to affix ourselves completely upon Christ.

Furthermore, only God knows when each of us will die. He knows the time of our deaths before we are even created. Job 14:5

clearly tells us this. *"Seeing his days are determined, the number of his months are with thee, thou hast appointed his bounds that he cannot pass."* Trust Jesus and follow Him. Allow God to determine how many days you will live.

That being said, the Bible never specifically says that suicide is an unforgiveable sin. Nothing can separate a true believer from God's love. The Apostle Paul reassures us of this twice in Romans 8, in 8:39 and in 8:1, when he writes, *"There is therefore now no condemnation to them which are in Christ Jesus, who walk not after the flesh, but after the Spirit."*

Jonah, a true believer, got so angry that he longed to die. Job suffered horribly and wretchedly, and he, too, wanted to die. However, God stayed with Job while Satan tortured him, and He blessed Job after the suffering ended. No one will ever suffer as did Jesus on the cross. We would understand had He begged God to end His life, but He never did that. Instead, He knew his fate was God's will. He bore that unimaginable pain for us, never seeking to escape the pain and torture. He suffered for us, so that our sin can be forgiven.

God never wants anyone to commit suicide, but He also understands that the human body and mind can endure only so much pain and suffering. A true Christian is assured of getting to Heaven when he dies, even if by suicide.

This statement shocked the COC members, for they had been told that all murder is wrong, as stated in the sixth Commandment. The first four Commandments direct us in our relationship with God. The remaining six Commandments instruct us in our relationships with other humans. None of them address how we treat ourselves. *"Thou shalt not kill"* (Exodus 20:13) refers to taking another person's life, not to suicide. Again, God does not condone suicide at all, but He never specifically states that it is an unforgiveable sin.

This discussion led to another important question: "Can any sin be forgiven?" The quick, short answer is no. Some people presume that the seven deadly sins cannot be forgiven, but that is false. These sins are discussed throughout scripture, although King

Solomon does mention them in Proverbs 6:16-19: "*These six things doth the Lord hate: yea, seven are an abomination unto him: A proud look, a lying tongue, and hands that shed innocent blood, An heart that deviseth wicked imaginations, feet that be swift in running to mischief, A false witness that speaketh lies, and he that soweth discord among brethren.*"

The seven deadly sins as we now identify them are lust (Matthew 5:28), gluttony (Proverbs 23:21), greed (Ephesians 4:19), sloth (Proverbs 115:19), wrath (Proverbs 15:1), envy (1 Peter 2:1-2), and pride (Proverbs 16:18). Although these sins are completely forgivable by God, this does not mean people should commit them. All sin displeases God.

However, He will forgive all but one sin if we repent and ask His forgiveness. In three separate Bible verses, Jesus Himself tells us which sin remains unforgiveable. Mark 3:28-29 and Luke 12:8-10 are two. In Matthew 12:31-32, Jesus declares, "*Wherefore I say to you, All manner of sin and blasphemy shall be forgiven unto men: but the blasphemy against the Holy Ghost shall not be forgiven unto men. And whosoever speaketh a word against the Son of man, it shall be forgiven him: but whosoever speaketh against the Holy Ghost, it shall not be forgiven him, neither in this world, nor in the world to come.*"

What does it mean to blaspheme the Holy Ghost? There is but one way: deny the Holy Ghost's witness to Jesus. Reject Christ.

Mark 3:29 calls it the eternal sin. Rejecting—denying—Jesus is the only unforgivable sin. As Stephen said in his sermon, recorded by Luke in Acts 7:51, "*Ye stiffnecked and uncircumcised in heart and ears, ye do always resist the Holy Ghost: as your fathers did, so do ye.*" Stephen convicted the congregation's Jewish leaders of killing Jesus Christ, just as their ancestors had persecuted God's prophets. The Jews to whom Stephen spoke had rejected the Savior whom the prophets had foretold. These Jews who demanded that the Romans crucify Jesus were descendants of Abraham, but they never truly believed that they would receive God's blessings only if they accepted Jesus Christ as their Savior. They denied Him. They committed the one unforgivable sin.

Most Christians who fear they have blasphemed the Holy Ghost live with the unwarranted angst of believing they aren't going to Heaven. Unwarranted? How? This is a very severe issue. Of course it is. However, most Christians do not deny Jesus as the Lord and Savior. Most do not give Lucifer credit for the Holy Ghost's work or praise Lucifer for their blessings. True Christians who do ask for God's forgiveness of their sins and claim Jesus Christ as their Savior will enter the gates of Heaven.

"What do the gates of Heaven look like?" Most depictions I saw when I lived on Earth showed gleaming, ornate golden gates that open wide when a soul is accepted into Heaven. These gates always reminded me of those I often saw at mansions, palaces, or even cemeteries. This is not what Heaven's gates look like, though.

The Apostle Paul tells us exactly what the gates of Heaven look like in Revelation, the book that came to him from Jesus via Gabriel. In Chapter 21, Verse 21, John writes, *"And the twelve gates were twelve pearls; every several gate was of one pearl: and the street of the city was pure gold, as it were transparent glass."* How glorious! Heaven contains all of God's Creations: gems, precious metals, trees, plants, and animals.

Yes, animals live in Heaven when their earthly lives end. After all, animals are the second most important inhabitants of Earth. God entrusts animals to our care and conservation. Furthermore, our relationships with animals form meaningful aspects of our lives.

Both the Old Testament and the New Testament assure us that animals dwell in Heaven. Isaiah 65:25 tells us that *"The wolf and the lamb shall feed together, and the lion shall eat straw like the bullock: and dust shall be the serpent's meat. They shall not hurt or destroy in all my holy mountain, saith the Lord."* The holy mountain is Heaven. This verse also proves that animals will no longer hunt and kill prey for food; their every need, like ours, is provided. There will never be any murder in Heaven for any reason, not even for food.

Job 12:10 reiterates this by telling us that, *"In whose hand is the soul of every living thing, and the breath of all mankind."* Every living being, human and animal, has a spirit, the breath of God.

The Apostle Paul, relaying Jesus' words, confirms that *"every creature which is in Heaven, and on earth, and under the earth, and such as are in the sea, and all that are in them, heard I saying, Blessing, and honour, and glory, and power, be unto him that sitteth upon the throne, and unto the Lamb for ever and ever"* (Revelation 5:13). Every creature will praise God in Heaven.

If my testimony counts, I, too, can comfort you that animals reside in Heaven. I have seen thousands, and even frequently witness lions, bears, and wolves sitting or walking alongside deer, zebras, and rabbits. Matthew often paints them. On a personal note, my beloved Palomino, Starlight, is here, as is my father's handsome stallion Midnight. We often ride them across the lush, green fields of Heaven. Heaven truly is more glorious than any words could ever convey.

Often in conversations with elderly, ill, or incapacitated people, I was asked why God kept them alive. They remained limited in what they could do, and they wanted to go to Heaven. God is quite aware of this desire, for the Apostle Paul writes in Philippians 1:23, *"For I am betwixt two, having a desire to depart, and to be with Christ; which is better."*

Do not feel guilty for asking God to take you to Heaven. Do realize, though, that He has reasons for keeping you on Earth. Ask Him to show you what His reasons are. *"They shall bring forth fruit in old age; they shall be fat and flourishing"* says Psalm 92:14. Age produces wisdom, experience, and maturity which can be productive.

Ask God to help you to be a witness for Him. Your life can become a powerful testimony, especially if you accept that God has a reason for keeping you on Earth. If you can show God's love and peace even in your situation, you will stand tall as a witness for God. You can help to bring others closer to God. As Paul wrote to Timothy, *"For therefore we both labour and suffer reproach, because we trust in the living God, who is the Saviour of all men, specially of those that believe"* (1 Timothy 4:10). Yes, I know how difficult it can be to maintain hope and peace when you hurt or suffer or feel despondent. I do.

Remember, though, that you are loved and valuable. You have a purpose, no matter how dire your circumstances may seem. Trust that God will remain with you and will use you to glorify Him. I once met an elderly woman named Maggie who lost her speech to a stroke that also debilitated her right side. Even though she could not speak, she continuously let people know how much God had done for her. Many people were shocked by that. Didn't God cause her stroke, after all? People asked her that. Her answer, written in shaky print with her non-dominant hand, was, "No. I caused my stroke. I made poor choices in my life that led me here. My fault. Not God's. But I am alive. I can watch my great-grandchildren grow. I can smell flowers. I can read my Bible. I can live for God. He has blessed me, even though I made many mistakes. When I do die, I will kiss His feet and thank Him." What a beautiful testimony!

This woman's story leads to a question I was often asked on Earth: "Will I see God?" No matter what else you do on Earth, the point is to put God first, to put Him into your heart and into your mind, and to let Him guide you. Live, respond to others, and work as a child of God. Let God shine forth in everything you do.

Will you see God when you enter Heaven? Yes! Jesus promises believers that we will see God face-to-face. In His Sermon on the Mount, Jesus proclaims eight blessings. *"Blessed are the pure in heart: for they shall see God"* (Matthew 5:8) is the sixth blessing He mentions.

We shall remain in continuous, unbroken fellowship and oneness with God, without the separation we have on Earth. Sin currently separates people from face-to-face contact with God. Once we enter those pearly gates of Heaven, we become sinless. Jesus, through the Apostle John, also assures us this in Revelation 21:3. *"And I heard a great voice out of heaven saying, Behold, the tabernacle of God is with men, and he will dwell with them, and they shall be his people, and God himself shall be with them, and be their God."* Amazing to ponder, right?

I have seen God. I have talked with Him. Nothing compares to seeing, to meeting, my Heavenly Father. I would never exist without Him, nor would I want to exist without God. My prayer is that you feel likewise, and that you will submit to Him. Open your heart, let God dwell there, claim Jesus as your Savior, and you will earn an eternal home in Heaven.

Why would you want to spend eternity elsewhere? Where else could you experience the deepest, truest love?

Love. Love is the heart of all of Creation. We were created from God's love. We are the manifestations of His love. The Earth upon which we live our physical lives was created from that same love, as a place that provides all we need in order to live those lives. Its beauty and wonder are manifestations of His love. Look around, and you will see His love in the sunrise, in a snowflake, in a soaring bird, in a majestic mountain, in a growing flower. Everything was created from that most perfect love.

So, too, was Heaven. God created Heaven as our eternal home. When we have finished our lives on Earth, and if we have reciprocated God's love for us, we will live in Heaven forevermore. Heaven is difficult to describe, for mere words can never capture the awesome wonder, beauty, and peace of Heaven. Heaven is the only place to ever exist where there is no strife, no pain, no sickness, no night, no hunger, no death, and no hatred. Love is all that exists in Heaven. Love fills Heaven and all who dwell here.

God's love for us fills Heaven and us. That love is so powerful and immense that there is no room for any other feeling. That love is the most comforting we will ever know. Heaven contains the most glorious beauty, beauty beyond human comprehension or imagination. True perfection exists only in Heaven, for Heaven is the only place untainted by the evils and ills that plague Earth.

You will never feel pain, sorrow, exhaustion, hunger, heartbreak, regret, anger, resentment. You will feel only peace, joy, and love. You will become a new creature made entirely of love. All of the baggage of your earthly life will leave you when you die and enter the gates of Heaven and begin your eternal life. You will still be you, but you will be reborn whole and perfect. Your physical life will end. Your spiritual life will never end. That is your reward for loving God as He loves you. No greater love exists than God's love for each of us, and Heaven is the proof of that love.

FOLLOWING IS A SCAN OF THE ORIGINAL MANUSCRIPT
HANDWRITTEN BY SAINT ANGILIA IN HEAVEN AND
DELIVERED TO HER GRANDSON PRINCE PATRICK

The Splendor of Heaven

Heaven. The most beautiful, loving place in existence. The most mystical, paradisiacal place humans contemplate. No other place evokes as much thought or inspires as many questions as does Heaven. Why?

The simple answer: Heaven is unknown. Anything unknown breeds interest and curiosity. More importantly, though, Heaven remains beyond human understanding. Heaven is unlike any place humans have ever seen or experienced. Heaven is far grander, far more beautiful, and far more peaceful than anywhere on Earth. Heaven arouses the human brain; Heaven challenges people's concepts, ideas, and images. Because Heaven truly is the only perfect place to ever exist, it is beyond anyone's ability to accurately and completely conceptualize.

No matter how many times we read the biblical descriptions of Heaven, we can never truthfully imagine its splendor. No place on Earth has ever rivaled Heaven. Our imagination—our ability to form images—is restricted by our earthly experiences. Sure, there exist beautiful, peaceful places on Earth. I lived in one—Valdavia. Of course beauty and peace exist on Earth; God created Earth, after all, as the home for our physical beings. God's glory remains evident in all of His Creation. However, the beauty and peace we do know can never prepare us for the awesome wonders of Heaven.

Heaven remains impossible for the human mind to fathom, because Heaven really is unlike anyplace else known to humankind. For hundreds of centuries, Earth has witnessed multiple wars, destructions, and crimes—all caused by humans. Universal peace and love have been sporadic, never permanent. Poverty, hunger, illness, murder, addiction, abuse, abandonment—these are what people on Earth live with daily. When faced with all of this, how can anyone be expected to visualize Heaven in all of its loving glory?

Neither can we see Heaven, not even through the most powerful telescope. Heaven is not a planet or a star.

Heaven is beyond anything the living can see, but that does not mean that Heaven is not real. On the contrary, Heaven is more real than the Earth, planets, and stars we do see and know. Furthermore, Heaven is eternal, and will remain long after the stars and galaxies cease to exist. 2 Peter 3:10 tells us that "The heavens [the planets and the stars] will disappear with a roar." As terrifying as that prospect seems for many people, rest assured that after we enter Heaven, we will be with God. No living being can fully comprehend what that is truly like, for it is far grander than any earthly experience. On Earth, things often go wrong, but in Heaven, all is perfect—because God is perfect. No evil exists in Heaven. God's perfection, holiness, and love protect us.

Moreover, Heaven exists in a dimension completely unlike anything those living on Earth can ever know. Earth is the temporary home of our physical beings; Heaven is the eternal home of our spiritual beings. When believers' physical bodies die, their souls enter Heaven and are reborn in new bodies. They enter a new level of existence and consciousness.

No, God does not erase all memories related to our earthly lives. Far from it. We do remember the people and moments that are connected to pleasant memories. Because negativity and evil do not exist in Heaven, all of our painful and negative memories leave us the exact second we enter Heaven. We are left with happiness, love, peace, and beauty—for all eternity. How wondrous that feels!

Other aspects of our earthly lives fall away, as well. Our spiritual bodies never crave sleep. In fact, our spiritual bodies are whole and healthy; all physical ailments we may have suffered on Earth die with our physical bodies. We still look the same, yet no longer are we restricted by any physical limitations. All of the trials and tribulations of our earthly lives pass away into nothingness. We will never even remember them.

All of this is quite difficult for humans to understand. No memories of anyone or anything painful or bad. No more disease, illness, or physical pain. Our earthly lives are filled with pain—emotional and physical—to the extent that we cannot fathom life without pain. What would that even feel like?

Free. Eternal life without pain is the freest life we can know. My friend Arthur Brennan, my Uncle Patrick, and I readily testify to that. When I met Mr. Brennan on January 3, 2012, he was in a wheelchair, to which he had been confined for nearly five years at that point. Mr. Brennan had suffered an accident that damaged his legs. While that never damaged his spirit, it did hamper his ability to do all of the things he had previously enjoyed: hiking, gardening, taking his dog for walks, and driving.

Upon his death in 2016, though, Mr. Brennan regained his mobility. His charming house in Heaven has a flower garden that both Mr. and Mrs. Brennan enjoy tending. They also enjoy leisurely walks over the verdant hills and valleys of Heaven. Often, they are joined by their dog Taffy, which delights Mr. Brennan. (Yes, animals dwell in Heaven. More on that later.)

My Uncle Patrick was 19 when he died in a boating accident on July 19, 1977. He suffered internal damage and a broken spine. He did not die instantly, which means he felt the most excruciating pain. Had he survived, he would have been paralyzed from the neck down. I was Uncle Patrick's Spirit Guide, the one chosen to escort his spiritual body to Heaven. Patrick walked alongside me as we climbed the invisible staircase to Heaven. Patrick has remained incredibly active in the 106 years since his death. As an envoy angel, Patrick is often sent to Earth on God's behalf. Patrick's most visible role has been as a singer and songwriter, with the purpose of proving life after death.

Patrick was my Spirit Guide when I died in 2069. We once again climbed that invisible staircase to Heaven. The moment I arrived, I did something I had not been able to do since 2012. I ran. I ran to my parents. My right knee had been permanently damaged by a bullet in March 2012. I walked with a pronounced limp for the rest of my life. My heart was also damaged in the shooting, and, in fact, heart failure caused my death. Since my rebirth, however, those physical ailments no longer affect my body. I run, I walk, I dance, and I even ride my pony Starlight at a full gallop. I am completely free, as are my Uncle Patrick and Mr. Brennan—and every other person who resides in Heaven.

Not only are we reborn in flawless spiritual bodies, but we live in perpetual daylight. Heaven is one eternal, perfect day. Night never occurs in Heaven, for there is no need for night. Heaven is light and all that light connotes: clarity, truth, revelation, goodness, purity, security, warmth, and love. Constant light, a light unlike any ever seen on Earth, brighter and warmer than sunlight. Heaven's light is the most exquisite light—because Heaven's light emanates from God Himself. God's essence and love light Heaven with a golden glow more powerful than any electrical grid could ever hope to mimic. Words cannot describe this light, but if a comparison will help, I offer mine. Heaven's light is like being wrapped in the safe, warm, loving embrace of a beloved parent. Fear and loneliness become alien concepts, forgotten feelings, when we enter Heaven and are surrounded by its light.

Why is there no night in Heaven? As I mentioned earlier, Heaven exists in its own dimension, one unknown to all who dwell outside it. Planets do not exist in Heaven's dimension. Because Heaven has no sun and no moon, there can be no night. Perpetual daytime—light—is as impossible to imagine as is most every aspect of Heaven. After all, on Earth we are used to the darkness that occurs when the sun sinks below the horizon. One side of Earth is always bathed in shadow. Heaven is never cloaked in shadow—what we call night.

There is no need for night in Heaven. On Earth, night is typically when most people sleep, relaxing our minds and our bodies, often promoting healing and health. First of all, those of us in Heaven never tire or feel sleepy. We exist in perpetual consciousness, alertness, and activity. Secondly, as already mentioned, we remain eternally healthy. Therefore, we have no need of sleep's restorative benefits. Imagine never feeling tired or exhausted, never craving a comfortable bed on which to drift into sleep.

In fact, none of the homes in Heaven contain bedrooms, beds, or lamps. Yes, we have our own homes in Heaven, each perfect and filled with happiness. Each home is unique, created by God to suit its occupants. Jesus promises us that "In my Father's house are many mansions. If it were not so, I would have told you. I go to prepare a place for you" (John 14:2). For example, Mr. and Mrs. Brennan live in a charming cottage, with a flower garden—complete with butterfly bushes. Ever since his infancy, Mr. Brennan enjoyed butterflies. In fact, his earliest memory is of trying to grab a butterfly in his mother's garden.

My in-laws, Mitchell and Katherine Taylor, have a lovely two-story home, where Katherine likewise has the flower garden she always wanted but never had the time to cultivate. Mitchell is content to sit on his rocking chair on the front porch, reading, visiting with family and friends, or engaging in a game of chess.

When Mitchell is not at home, he indulges in his favorite sport, golf. Since doctors aren't needed in Heaven, Mitchell has more time for golf. A golf course exists near his home. Mr. Brennan, my Uncle Eduardo, and many others join Mitchell. There is no competition as on Earth, though, only pure fun and enjoyment.

In fact, we all have the freedom to partake in what we enjoyed doing on Earth. Matthew draws and paints. I write books and music. Uncle Patrick plays sports. Katherine gardens. My father helps people.

Heaven is not all fun and games, though. We never slide into slothfulness. Everyone works, including God and Jesus. Jesus tells us so in John 5:17. "My Father worketh hitherto, and I work." We plant, cultivate, and harvest food for the heavenly feasts and celebrations. We tend to the animals and children. As our earthly work should, our heavenly work honors God.

My beloved parents' home is large, fittingly so. Many people frequently gather there. I rejoice every time I visit their home, for of course I cherish being with them, but I also truly enjoy talking with my ancestors—those whom I never had the chance to know. On Earth, genealogy remained a vitally important component of my life from early childhood. I maintained a huge family history book filled with facts, stories, and pictures of ancestors dating back to biblical times. When I lived on Earth, I knew I would meet my ancestors in Heaven, and I have. I longed for and looked forward to knowing them and talking with them. How wonderful to do so whenever I desire.

The first relative I met was my great-grandfather, Stefan DeBruce Martineau, when Archangel Michael brought me to the Third Sphere of the Angel Realm from the Unborn Children Sphere. Great-grandfather is a wise, kind man, and he taught me much in my time there. I did not know at the time that he was preparing me to become my uncle's Spirit Guide. Because of my role, Uncle Patrick was the second relative I knew.

Uncle Patrick's home is essentially a studio apartment—one large room. Patrick is rarely there, though, for he remains constantly active, mostly playing sports or singing when he isn't carrying out his duties as an envoy angel. When he is home, he either reads or writes, betraying the dunce image he cultivated in his teens. On Earth, Patrick hid his intelligence, introspection, and creativity as much as he could. Sensitive, poetry-writing teen boys faced teasing and bullying, and Patrick never wanted any of that to overshadow or interfere with his public role.

Since Patrick had been born a Prince de Valdavia, he performed frequent public duties and appointments. He enjoyed meeting people. More than that, he relished helping people, as well as encouraging or motivating them. While Patrick attended middle school, he became active in the

Scout Guides, a national organization for children. His first official patronage was with the Athletic Association of Valdavia, which fostered and supported sports throughout the nation.

Patrick had been involved in sports most of his life, and while he was in high school he found his favorite sport—speed boat racing. He never intended that to be his career, though. His goal and desire was to become a career soldier in the Valdavian Army. Patrick had just begun that career and become a plebe when he died in the speed boat accident.

Now, in Heaven, Patrick frequently talks with athletes and soldiers, still pursuing his favorite subjects: physical fitness and international security. Patrick's primary goal as a soldier was to prevent war rather than to fight and kill people. He longed to promote and to educate every nation about peace. Patrick firmly believes that peace is attainable on Earth, and his earthly life would have been dedicated to that mission.

Like Uncle Patrick, Matthew and I do not stay at our home very often. We take walks or sit alongside a brook, talking, writing, and drawing. We visit family, friends, and welcome newcomers to Heaven. Sometimes we ride Starlight together; Matthew is no longer skittish of horses, as he was on Earth. When we are at our home, which is a delightful cottage reminiscent of the one in which Snow White found refuge, we do just as we did long ago in the Unborn Children Sphere. Matthew draws or paints, and I play the piano or write. Otherwise, we snuggle on the sofa, sometimes talking but often contently silent.

Words have long been unnecessary for Matthew and me to communicate. From the beginning of our friendship, we possessed an intuitive understanding of one another. Comfortable silence endures as one of our relationship's gifts. The love, support, and compassion we have shared for centuries allow us to dwell in tranquility, solidarity, and affection.

Matthew and I are kindred souls in every way; neither of us romantically loved another. Our union was predestined.

My first consciousness is being in a beautiful, large, gold limestone temple, which I learned was the Unborn Children Sphere. The Unborn Children Sphere exists in the same dimension as Heaven and the Angel Realm. Peace dominates all of Heaven, and from the beginning of my existence, I felt the serenity and joy of that peace.

As I began walking, I saw these unborn souls doing whatever they were destined to perform on Earth. Orators practiced speeches at podiums. Scientists conducted experiments in laboratories. Astronomers studied Earth's planetary system through telescopes. Teachers conducted lessons in classrooms. Artists drew and painted. Musicians performed on various instruments peppered throughout the temple. Writers drafted manuscripts at desks. How marvelous, I thought, to have our lives' paths planned for us and to be able to hone our skills. I wondered what my destiny was as I wandered.

As I passed a massive bookshelf, I removed a book of poetry and began climbing a winding staircase. More unborn children greeted me as I ascended, and I smiled continuously. Everyone treated me with benevolence, and I instantly knew I was where I belonged—I was home. That feeling grew stronger once I entered the tower at the top of the staircase.

A piano and one boy were there, nothing and no one else. I walked closer to him, and he looked up and smiled at me. "You are new here. Welcome. I will be your friend."

"I would like that. My name is Angilia."

"Hello, Angilia. I am Matthew. Sit here beside me."

I did, and noticed a sketch book in his hand and colored pencils and paints on the floor. "You are an artist. May I see your work?" He showed me some drawings and watercolors of the Unborn Children Sphere and some of the unborn children. "These are beautiful, Matthew."

"Thank you. What book do you have?" I handed him the book, and he opened the pages and leafed through them.

"Poetry. Would you mind reading some poems aloud while I draw? Please?"

I nodded, and read the first poem I opened to, Epic of Gilgamesh, the oldest written epic poem, composed in approximately 2100 B.C. I read several other poems, engrossed in the beauty of the words, images, similes, and ideas.

When I stopped, Matthew gently put his hand on my arm and looked at me with an expression I of course had never before seen. "You read poetry with such emotion and passion, Angilia. Even your face as you read reflected the emotions of the poems. I could not stop watching you as you read. Thank you for this experience."

I was speechless for a moment. Everything was new to me. "You are welcome, but I distracted you from your drawing."

"Not at all, Angilia. Because of you, I have drawn my most beautiful subject."

"Really? You drew an interpretation of one of the poems?"

"No." Matthew held his sketch book toward me. "You."

"Me? You drew me?" He smiled and nodded as I looked at my image. "I look like this? It feels odd to see myself."

"Yes, this is how you look, perfectly beautiful and angelic. I have met thousands of children here, Angilia, and I have never seen eyes that resemble yours, so intense, expressive, and that shade of blue."

"Really? So I am unlike the others here? Why?"

"Everyone here is unique, but most have similarities. Many children have blonde hair, as you do, but I have never seen that particular blonde before. Many have blue eyes, but not the same blue as yours. Your eyes are like the blue of a river or an ocean. You are unlike any other child here, yes, but I do not believe that is negative. After all, each of us was created by God, right?"

I smiled at Matthew. "Right. Matthew, I have never seen a river or an ocean. What do they look like?" I asked him. I learned something every minute.

Matthew stood and reached for my hand. "Come," he smiled, and led me down the staircase and into a room. An art gallery. As I glanced all around, Matthew guided me to a painting and suddenly stopped. "This is a beach with an ocean and mountains. See the blue of the water? Your eyes are that color, the color of the ocean."

"Oh," I gasped. I had only seen myself as he had drawn me with his colored pencils. He had made my eyes that color. "The ocean looks beautiful but very powerful. Did you paint this, Matthew?"

"No. One of the envoy angels did after a visit to Earth."

"Envoy angels? Earth? I feel so ignorant. I know nothing."

Matthew giggled. "You are not ignorant. None of us knew anything when we first arrived as baby souls, either.

We all must learn, Angilia." Matthew explained envoy angels and Earth to me, and I began to understand.

"Will I ever meet an envoy angel?" I asked him.

"Perhaps. They sometimes come here to visit us."

I never met an envoy angel in the Unborn Children Sphere, but I sure did come to dearly love one—my Uncle Patrick!

Although I never met an envoy angel, I met others in the Unborn Children Sphere. You see, some souls remain there for what humans understand as hundreds of years before their earthly lives begin—before they are born to their parents.

While everyone I met is distinctive and memorable, some stand out in my memory, but not because I knew then the lives they would endure on Earth. Even prior to their physical births, these souls touched me deeply. My memories of these encounters remain vivid and detailed.

These encounters confirm that God creates every human being righteous. God creates each of us in His image, as

Moses writes in Genesis 1:27: "So God created man in his own image, in the image of God created he him: male and female he created them." No, humans do not inherit God's flesh and bone; we cannot be physical children of God, because God is Spirit. However, Adam and Eve mirrored God. They were created in perfect health and gifted with immortality. Humankind was further provided reason and choice, which reflect God's intellect and freedom. Humans inherited God's likeness mentally, morally, and socially.

However, humans now also bear the imperfection of sin. Because God gives us choice—free will—we have the freedom to do as we please. We do not have to obey God, even though that is His wish for us. He intends our conscience to guide us into remaining "very good" (Genesis 1:31). Adam scarred the image of God within himself when he chose to disobey God. That scar has dwelt in every human since Adam.

All of us commit sin at some point in our earthly lives, but God promises redemption through our faith in Jesus Christ as His Son and our Savior (Ephesians 2:8-9). God understands that all humans stumble and fall, but He does not forsake anyone. Those who forsake Him, however, lose all hope of redemption and an eternal home in Heaven.

Once, Matthew was painting one of the rooms in the Unborn Children Sphere, one with curved walls, leveled floors, nooks, and—as do all rooms there—paneless windows. His easel stood in the center of the room, and he painted every feature of the room.

I stood watching him, and after a while, I sketched Matthew at work. As I watched him and drew, I noticed someone beside me. He looked from Matthew to me and smiled. "An artist drawing an artist. Two kindred souls. May I watch, too?"

"Of course. Matthew is an incredible artist."

The young man stood on his toes, leaned to the left, and studied Matthew's painting. "Yes. He is. His perspective, balance, and shadowing are expert. His depiction of this room is lifelike."

"You know art. Are you an artist?"

"Yes, I am. I paint or draw anything or anyone I see. I think I am good." He bowed his head, looked at me, and smiled. "That is vain, I suppose, and wrong here."

"God made us, and He gave us the abilities we have. We should use them. When we do, it honors Him. He should remain the focus. We would have nothing without Him." I replied.

"Yes, I suppose. But if He gave us a skill, are we not inherently exceptional at it?"

His question unsettled me. "Not necessarily. Our duty is to refine and polish that skill. God gifts us the ability to do something, but it is up to us to develop that and to become proficient at it. Not everyone does, so, no, not everyone is exceptionally talented."

"So if I desire to be the best, I need to draw and paint often? I need to practice. Is that right?"

"Yes. Matthew's work is so realistic because he draws and paints habitually. He has perfected his techniques. You should speak with Matthew. The two of you can work together sometimes."

"I would like that." He looked down at my sketchbook. "May I draw with you?"

"Of course you may."

"I would like to paint you. May I?" He paused. "What are you called?"

"Angilia. And, yes, you may, if you want."

He bowed. "I am indebted, Angilia."

I quickly studied my new friend. He was not tall, and he was rather pale. His dark brown hair was parted to one side and flat against his head. His eyes were blue, but a pale blue. How he stared through me. I had never seen an expression like his before, so penetrating and intense. I saw that many times in historic film footage and photographs during my earthly life. So have many of you, I'm sure.

Not long after our first meeting, Adolf and Matthew painted together for the first time. They asked me to accompany them, so I followed and sat in a window watching them. A cherub from the Angel Realm served as the subject of their painting.

Matthew and Adolf set up their easels next to one another, as they both wanted as close to the same perspective as possible. As the cherub played a flute, Matthew and Adolf sketched and then painted the cherub. When they both finished, the cherub waved and then winged its way back to the Angel Realm.

Each of them studied the other's painting, and each praised the other. Soon, others came by and commented that both paintings were true-to-life and expertly executed. Matthew smiled at Adolf, who blushed and appeared moved.

"Everyone is correct. Both of your paintings are well accomplished. In fact, they are almost identical except for your individual, unique brush strokes. Both of these will embellish the walls of the Sphere, and through them, both of your souls' imprints will remain here," I commented as I stood between Matthew and Adolf.

"I will like that, even if I never remember the Sphere," Adolf smiled.

"So will I," Matthew added.

"I still want to paint you, Angilia," Adolf reminded me.

Matthew suggested he do so right then since his easel and paints were prepared. So he did. I sat in the window again, and Matthew watched Adolf paint me. When he finished, Adolf stepped aside and asked Matthew, "Have I captured your fair maiden?"

Matthew stared at the painting. "Absolutely. May I keep this in the tower where I spend much of my time?"

"You may," Adolf bowed. "I hope I may visit you both there."

We assured Adolf he could, and Matthew carried the canvas to the tower. Once there, he leaned the painting against a wall and whispered, "I am glad we met Adolf."

"So am I, Matthew. Adolf should accomplish many honorable acts on Earth. I hope we somehow learn all he does accomplish. Chances are, we will not live on Earth at the same time as Adolf."

"I know." Matthew took my hand. "We are all meant to accomplish things. We all have a reason for our lives. We know that. Perhaps we will receive information about those we meet here, though we will not remember them once we are born."

"I know. But I can never anticipate forgetting you, Matthew."

"Nor I you."

Of course I never forgot Matthew—or anyone I met in the Unborn Children Sphere. When I was four and first saw a World War Two-era photograph of the Führer of Germany and Leader of the Nazi Party, I recognized him instantly. I asked my father if he knew anything about Adolf, and what I learned saddened me and hurt my heart. The kind, friendly Adolf I had known before our earthly lives became one of the cruelest, most amoral people. God is not responsible for Adolf's actions; Adolf chose the path he trod. He chose to forsake God. In fact, he claimed that he did not believe in God.

Adolf's story remains a perfect illustration of what it means to deny God and what that leads one toward. Another meeting Matthew and I had in the Sphere exemplifies the juxtaposition of Adolf's story. Once when Matthew and I walked down the winding staircase from our tower, I saw a young man sitting alone in a chair, bent over reading a book. I grabbed Matthew's hand and went to the man, and he looked up at us with his thin-lipped, kind smile.

He greeted us and shook our hands. Matthew and I introduced ourselves. The man stood and bowed. He was quite tall, probably as tall as my Uncle Patrick, and he is six feet three inches tall. As he stood from his bow, he said, "I am pleased to meet you, Angilia and Matthew. I am Abraham."

His dark hair was mussed, and when he ran his hand through it a few times, I knew why. We talked to him for a while, and he read aloud from the book he held. I never forgot the stanza he read, and I looked it up once in my father's library. Abraham read to us the Epitaph of Thomas Gray's poem "Elegy Written in a Country Churchyard."

Here rests his head upon the lap of Earth

A youth to Fortune and to Fame unknown.

Fair Science frown'd not on his humble birth,

And Melancholy mark'd him for her own.

Large was his bounty, and his soul sincere.

Heav'n did a recompense as largely send:

He gave to Mis'ry all he had, a tear,

He gain'd from Heav'n ('twas all he wish'd) a
    friend.

No farther seek his merits to disclose.

Or draw his frailties from their dread abode,

(There they alike in trembling hope repose)

The bosom of his Father and his God.

    Abraham said something a moment later that I never forgot. He sat in the chair again, rested his arm on the back of the chair, and looked at the poem for a short while before he closed the book and left it on his lap. He took our hands in his, gave us a sad smile, and said, "I dare but hope people will think of me and remember me with the tenderness and truth of these lines. I can only pray that whatever I am meant to do on Earth will meet the trust and responsibility placed upon me, my dears."

I recollect feeling so incredibly despondent for the first time in my existence, and Matthew put his hand on my back, as he often did during our marriage, to soothe me. Abraham pulled me to him and held me while I cried. After a long while, he told me, "Angilia, please do not cry for me. Whatever my path through life, I will do what I must. I will live my destiny. So shall you." He kissed my cheek, pulled me away from his shoulder, and winked at me. "When you do think of me, know that no matter how difficult or full of despair my life, I did the best I could. You will go to Earth long after I return to Heaven, but we will meet again someday, my dear."

Abraham lived a life guided by the Bible and prayer. Yes, he was murdered for his beliefs and actions, but he died knowing he had lived the life intended for him. The entire world knows Abraham as the 16th President of the United States. He was correct, of course. We have reconnected in Heaven.

There is one more encounter in the Unborn Children Sphere which proves that God plans our lives long before we are created. I wrote about this meeting on November 17, 2001, my father's 47th birthday; I was five years old. Here is what I wrote, primarily for my father, although I also shared this with my husband Matthew when I became pregnant.

"Daddy, someday you will read my diary about my life in the Unborn Children Sphere and the Angels Choir. You will know that I met a boy named Matthew in the Unborn Children Sphere, a boy who loves art and who was my best friend. I never forgot him. I never will. You know that Great-grandfather was my teacher in the Angels Choir and that he helped me learn about and prepare for my purpose there. You know that my purpose was to be Uncle Patrick's Spirit Guide, and I pray that the memory of that day no longer causes you pain. It shouldn't. Uncle Patrick is still around, Daddy, and someday you will see him, too. I know that. Seeing you the day I came to escort Uncle Patrick to Heaven remains the one most earth-shattering experience for me. I loved you at first sight, Daddy. I hope you know that.

"I met someone else in the Unborn Children Sphere who changed my life before I saw you, though. I will never forget him. I never could. Someday I will see him again. I know that. So will you. I know that, too.

"Once when I walked down the winding staircase from my and Matthew's tower, I instantly saw a man across the room. He saw me at the same moment. Our eyes locked. I felt odd, like I had to go to him, like I was compelled to walk across the room to him. He drew me to him as if he had lassoed and pulled me to him.

"There is no age in the Unborn Children Sphere. Everyone takes on the physical manifestation of what they will look like on Earth, although everyone appears to be what we know as different ages. Some of the unborn children I met there appeared to be five years old, while others appeared to be in their 20s or 30s. It's different for everyone. I asked Michael about that once, when I was in the Angels Choir, and he told me that some people in the Unborn Children Sphere parallel the ages they will be on Earth during major events in their lives.

"Maybe that is why I call the person I met a man, not a boy. He appeared to be in his 40s perhaps, like some of the diplomats who visit who are in that age range. That means something major will happen in his life during that time. I wonder what it will be. I honestly have no idea, although I wonder if we will witness that event, Daddy. It's within possibility.

"I walked to the man and felt so startled when I looked at him and into his eyes. His eyes amazed me. His eyes looked like my eyes. No one else I met in the Unborn Children Sphere had eyes that resembled mine. There were quite a lot of people there with blue eyes, but no one else with turquoise eyes. I never saw anyone else with these eyes until I came for Uncle Patrick and saw you, Daddy. I have your eyes. So does the man I met in the Unborn Children Sphere.

"He smiled at me, and I felt strange. I can now describe how I felt. My heart fluttered. It did so again when he pulled me into a hug and held me tight for a long while. Something about him seemed so familiar, warm, and honest. I loved him at that moment. That seems odd, I know, since I had just seen him for the first time and not spoken with him yet. I loved him instantly. I don't know how else to explain how I felt, and I hope that makes sense.

"He finally spoke, as he still held me to him. He was much taller than I was, but he held me close to him and said, 'I love you so very much. I never thought I would see you until my birth. You are all I imagined you to be'.

"I looked up at him, and I am sure my face betrayed my confusion. He took my hand and led me to a settee away from everyone else, where we could talk alone. He smiled and held my hands. 'You do not know who I am, do you, Angilia?" He knew my name, and my heart fluttered again when he said my name. I felt as though I recognized him, even though I had never seen him before. I knew I loved him.

"I'm not sure. I feel as if we have known each other forever, and yet I have never seen you before. I do love you. I know that."

He smiled at me and pulled me close to him again. "I love you, too, so very much. We will know each other for all time. We met here, but we will meet again on Earth in the future. You and I are meant to be together, part of the same soul." He looked into my eyes, and suddenly I knew. I knew who he is, who he will always be.

He nodded as he looked deep into my eyes, into my soul's depth. I placed my hand over his cheek, and it was as if an electric shock went through my whole being. "I do know you." I whispered. "You are my son, my only child."

"Yes. You are my mother. I am your son. You know me. I know you. You are my mother Angilia. I am your son Eric. You love me. I love you. That is how it is and will be for all eternity. We are meant to be mother and son. God placed us together, and thus it will always be. I love you. Carry that with you while you await my arrival."

"I nodded, and we hugged. He kissed my cheek. We sat together for what seemed like a long time. I never saw him again, for it seemed not long after that meeting with Eric that Michael came to take me to the Angels Choir. I somehow feel I will give birth to him in my mid-20s.

"I never forgot Eric. How could I? I never told anyone about him, though. This is the first I have mentioned him at all."

Our births and deaths are established by God when He creates us. Only He determines the dates and times of our births and deaths. He may not always control the circumstances of our deaths, though, because God has no dominion over those who choose to commit violent or careless acts that cause people's deaths. My Uncle Patrick is a prime example of God's plan. Patrick was born on January 6, 1958, and he died on July 19, 1977. He was 19 years old. Patrick's lifespan had been decided when God created his soul.

God always meant for Patrick to die on July 19, 1977, but God did not cause the speed boat accident that killed Patrick. Had Patrick not gone speed boating that day, he would have died in another manner. Why would God want someone to die at only 19? God had a much grander purpose for Patrick, one that Patrick has lived since his physical death. Patrick has served God as an envoy angel, spreading the truth of eternal life. Everything Patrick has done—the recordings, public appearances, interviews—is with God's blessing and to serve God.

Each of us has a purpose, a reason for being created—the reason we exist. God has a plan for our lives. Our duty is to open ourselves up to that purpose and to fulfill that during our earthly lives. Not everyone does that, of course; some people forge their own paths in life.

Our purpose is not directly tied to our job titles, educations, deeds, or relationships. These should all play roles in fulfilling our purpose, however. God's will for each of His children is that we follow His heart, allowing Him to fill us and work through us every moment of our lives on Earth. He desires us to develop an intimate relationship with His Son, Jesus. He wants us to commit to Jesus, for in doing so, we commit to our lifelong mission. Luke wrote Jesus' words in Acts 1:8. "But ye shall receive power, after that the Holy Ghost is come upon you: and ye shall be witness unto me both in Jerusalem, and in all Judea, and in Samaria, and unto the uttermost part of the earth." We are called to witness for Jesus.

If we allow the story of our lives to unfold as we connect with Jesus—the Word—we live the life intended for us. Everything we do aligns with that. In fact, the why of our existence begins with the heart, as stated by Solomon in

Proverbs 4:24. "Keep thy heart with all diligence: for out of it are the issues of life." We must guard our hearts, and our minds, for these (emotion and logic) guide everything we do.

God furthermore desires three things of us. One is that His followers are faithful to Him. Another is that parents nurture their children in righteousness. Lastly, He desires that His Word—the Truth—spread to every nation. Samuel wrote, "And I will raise me up a faithful priest, that shall do according to that which is in mine heart and in my mind: and I will build him a sure house; and he shall walk before mine anointed for ever" (1 Samuel 2:35). Do what is in God's heart and mind: align your heart and mind with God's. God's true purpose for each of us is to live for Him and to honor Him in all we do.

How each of us does so is not important necessarily. People do so through art, literature, serving food, music, teaching, sweeping floors and sundry other occupations. We can honor God no matter our jobs. He has no regard for titles and awards. His concern is how we live for Him and serve Him in all we do.

Anytime someone asked me about the meaning of life, I thought of Paul Gauguin's 1897 painting. Gauguin wrote three questions in the upper left corner:

D'où Venons Nous

Que Sommes Nous

Où Allons Nous

The first question, Where do we come from?, is easy to answer. We all come from God. He creates every living being.

Question two relates to the first question. What are we? We are souls. We begin existence as souls in the Unborn Children Sphere. When we are born, our souls inhabit physical bodies, which are temporary homes for our souls. Upon our deaths, the physical bodies are no longer needed. Our souls exist for all eternity.

Where are we going? Gauguin's third question has two possible answers: Heaven or Hell. Those whose faith and belief in God remain firmly implanted throughout their earthly lives, those who live according to God's laws, spend eternity in Heaven with God. Those who reject the Holy Ghost spend eternity in Hell with Lucifer.

Lucifer remains the prime example of one who begins as a child of God, imbued with His love. Lucifer was the second most beautiful being in Heaven: God is the most beautiful. Lucifer sat at God's right hand, a place of honor. He was loved. He was trusted. Even his name indicates God's feelings for him—it means 'Light Bearer.' Lucifer was magnificent. Lucifer was an archangel, along with Michael.

However, even angels are endowed with free will. Lucifer became unsatisfied with the honors and blessings bestowed upon him. Sitting beside God and being the second most beautiful being in Heaven were not enough for him. Lucifer became jealous of God. He desired God's dominion. He wanted to rule Heaven, to usurp God. We all know that a battle ensued. Lucifer convinced other angels to follow him, and they became his unholy army. Michael and his army of angels outnumbered and overpowered Lucifer.

As a result, God granted Lucifer dominion over a kingdom—Hell. Lucifer reigns, and his legion of fallen angels serve him. Hell is truly dark, fiery, and full of unimaginable torment. We read one example of this in Luke 16:22-26: "And it came to pass, that the beggar died, and was carried by the angels into Abraham's bosom: the rich man also died, and was buried; And in hell he lift up his eyes, being in torments, and seeth Abraham afar off, and Lazarus in his bosom. And he cried and said, Father Abraham, have mercy on me, and send Lazarus, that he may dip the tip of his finger in water, and cool my tongue; for I am tormented in this flame. But Abraham said, Son, remember that thou in thy lifetime receivedst thy good things, and likewise Lazarus evil things: but now he is comforted, and thou art tormented. And beside all this, between us and you there is a great gulf fixed: so that they which would pass from hence to you cannot; neither can they pass to us, that would come from thence." This passage proves that those in Hell can see Heaven and its glories. What greater anguish than to see the love, peace, and beauty of Heaven while suffering amidst the intense flames of Hell?

But where is Hell? Do we know? Yes. God tells us in Matthew 12:40 that "For as Jonas was three days and three nights in the whale's belly; so shall the Son of man be three days and three nights in the heart of the earth." Hell is at the center of the Earth. Hell is a place of separation and punishment.

Yes, Jesus spent the time between His Crucifixion and His Resurrection in Hell. Why? Jesus' death paid the price for our sins; His blood remains our salvation. After He died on the cross, Jesus went to Hell to prove His triumph over death and sin, as stated in Colossians 2:15: "And having spoiled principalities and powers, he made a show of them openly, triumphing over them in it." Before He departed Hell, Jesus took "the keys of hell and death" from

Lucifer, the devil (Revelation 1:18). This act further solidifies the truth that those who are saved by Jesus' blood can never truly die and are protected from Hell.

That does not mean we are never tempted or persecuted by Lucifer. We are, for he is relentless in his determination to claim as many souls as possible. Lucifer will say or do anything in order to seduce people away from God. He tried to tempt Jesus, as told to us in Matthew 4:1-11.

Just as he came to Jesus, Lucifer visited me once. On July 13, 2013, I was working in the basement recording studio. I had just finished recording a demo of a new song, and the studio became extremely cold. I knew instantly that Uncle Patrick wasn't visiting, because angel manifestations generate warmth. Coldness indicates evil spirits. Whose, though?

Before I had a chance to think further, strong, cold hands grabbed my shoulders. I knew immediately, for only one being could be that chillingly cold. "Lucifer," I stated.

"Why are you here? You know that you are not welcome here."

"And why is that? I once sat on God's right hand."

I turned to face him. "Once, yes. Past tense. You chose to end that, to forsake your seat of honor. You had beauty, wisdom, talent, and perfection, yet you wanted more. You wanted to be worshipped like God. Your greed and ego brought you down. You turned against God, who had created you in love and who had gifted you and honored you above all others."

"Whose ego is greater? God refuses to share His glory, His power, His dominion. He is greedy, seeking to be worshipped more than anyone else."

"He is the sole Creator. He gives life to everyone and everything. He asks for our faith, loyalty, and worship in return for the gifts he bestows upon us." I countered calmly yet assertively.

Lucifer laughed, a deep guttural sound I have never again heard. "Gifts? He let you nearly be killed by an assassin's bullet, and yet you defend Him."

"No. God had nothing to do with the shooting. Gregor Jamieson had, like you, turned his back on God; he chose to follow you instead. You are responsible for Jamieson's actions. You. Why? Because my father and I believe in and worship God?" I saw a smile form on his black lips. "My father and I are not afraid of death. As children of God who obey Him, we are both confident that we will be welcomed into Heaven when our earthly lives end. Even if I had died last year, I would be with God in Heaven, not with you in Hell."

"How can you be sure, Angilia, angel girl?"

"Because God and His Son Jesus tell me so." I looked at Lucifer, once so very beautiful and now so unutterably vile. "God made us and He named us. Your name Lucifer means Light Bearer." You were the son of the morning. Now you are pure darkness. And for what? To reign over Hell for all eternity? Those who follow you and dwell in Hell no longer praise you once they are there, do they? They curse you for luring them to eternal torture. How proud you must feel."

"Do not mock me! How would you know what Hell is like?"

"Hell is the antithesis of Heaven."

"Hell is my domain, my kingdom. Come, you will have an honor no living soul has been granted. You, Angilia, will visit Hell and see my kingdom for yourself."

Lucifer pulled me to him, held me tight, and departed through the floor and palace foundation. Alice's spiral down the rabbit hole could never be as surreal as my journey with Lucifer. In mere seconds, he sped through the ground to the center of Earth—to Hell. Heat assaulted me immediately. The only refuge from the total darkness was the light from the fires. It took several moments for my eyes to adjust.

My senses were also assaulted. I felt the heat. I smelled burning flesh. I saw dead souls writhing in agony and attempting to escape the fiery pits. I heard the moans, screams, and pleas of thousands of souls, some of whom begged God to save them. My heart ached. They had denied God during their earthly lives, but they sought His comfort once confronted with the reality of their eternal damnation.

Lucifer seemed to sense my thoughts. He took me to the precipice of the pit and forced me to look closely. Several poor souls reached for Lucifer and begged him to release them from the pit. He laughed that disturbing cackle in response.

One man reached up at me, and he actually cried. "You are not one of us. Did you come to save us? Please save me."

I shook my head. "No. I cannot save any of you. You brought yourselves here." He asked how. "You denied God as your Creator and His Son Jesus as your Savior.

This is your sentence. There is nothing I can do but pray for your master."

"Pray for me?" Lucifer asked through clenched teeth. "Why? God can do nothing for me any longer."

"Yes, He can, Lucifer. You loved God once. He still loves you. If you could put away your pride and earnestly ask His forgiveness, He will grant it." He looked into my eyes, silent but attentive.

"You were the most beautiful angel He created. Even Michael says so. Michael told me about you, about you as the Chief Covering angel who was very close to God. You were cloaked in gold and jewels. Somewhere deep in your soul that Lucifer still exists. He can reclaim you. Let him. Let go of your pride and anger."

As I spoke, I saw something hopeful glimmer in his dark eyes: longing. Then he slightly recoiled, and it disappeared. He once more appeared haughty. "How dare you presume to know me? What makes you think I would ask for God's forgiveness?"

I looked into his eyes. "So that you can reclaim what you once were and had: a beloved, trusted archangel seated alongside God in His throne room."

That longing briefly flitted through him, but he once more denied it. "His throne room, not mine. Why would I want to be second to anyone, when here I have my own throne?"

"Why would you not? Why spend eternity in this dark, burning abyss of torture? Why not return to light, love, and peace?"

"Why allow my Creator to force me into subservience? Why was I not given power and dominion? Why would I be God's lapdog, when I can rule over my own kingdom?"

"Are you happy here?"

"Happy? I do not need happiness. I have what I want here."

"I'm sorry," I said. Lucifer raged, and he shoved me. A hand from the fiery pit grabbed my leg, and I looked down—and gasped. "Gregor Jamieson." I had last seen him more than one year earlier, the day he committed suicide.

"I can still have my revenge. Let me torture her to death," he begged Lucifer.

"You cannot hurt me any longer. You have no power over me, Gregor Jamieson. Neither you nor the fires of Hell can harm me. I belong to God, and He protects me."

Jamieson smirked and pulled me into the pit. The whole of Hell trembled, as if shaken by an earthquake. God's wrath.

"Let her go!" Lucifer commanded. "Now!"

Jamieson did let go of me, but he did not lift me out of the pit. I struggled to climb out, and I felt many hands on me as the condemned grabbed me. Were they trying to hold me in the pit? Were they trying to leave with me? I will never know. As Hell rattled again, Lucifer betrayed fear. He reached down and lifted me from the pit.

"Do not forget my kingdom, Angilia."

"I won't. I will tell people how wretched and deplorable Hell is."

Lucifer appeared offended. Had he really expected me to find Hell appealing and welcoming? How could I do that? Hell truly is the opposite of Heaven.

Without another word, Lucifer took me home, back to the recording studio. As he turned to leave, I put my hand on his arm and said, "I will pray for you, Lucifer." He never looked at me, but he nodded once.

Yes, Lucifer did feel regret for his rebellion, but his pride kept him from asking God for forgiveness. Lucifer had to want a return to his former seat of honor in Heaven. I would pray that he open his heart to God once again

I continue to pray for Lucifer, but thus far he has remained steadfast in his separation from God. I have never seen him since that day, yet I pray that I do—not the Lucifer the world knows as Satan, but the Lucifer who was the shining archangel.

Other angels from the Archangel Choir whom I met while in the Unborn Children Sphere and the Angel Realm include Gabriel and Michael. Gabriel is God's supreme divine messenger or envoy angel, and he was sent by God to Zacharias and Mary. Gabriel has a special affinity to parents and children, creators, and the arts.

Gabriel is the angel above all other angels who was sent to Zacharias to inform him that his infertile wife Elizabeth would give birth to a very special boy named John. Luke 1:3 tells us that Elizabeth was barren, but God opened her womb for John, who would precede his cousin.

John's cousin's mother received a divine visit from Gabriel six months later. Mary, a relative of Elizabeth, was young, unmarried, and dwelt in Nazareth. She never questioned or doubted Gabriel when he told her that she would give birth to God's Son, Jesus, as related in Luke 1:26-27.

Gabriel was chosen by God to deliver these most important of messages to Zacharias and Mary. We know Elizabeth's son as John the Baptist, the young man who baptized his cousin Jesus. Gabriel was entrusted with another major task. He sent the book of Revelation to the Apostle John, as stated in Revelation 1:1-2.

Gabriel, like all of God's supreme angels, is remarkably beautiful, fair and golden-haired. Gabriel is my musical partner, beginning in the Angels Choir and now in Heaven. We play piano duets, often accompanied by angels playing violins, harps, and horns.

Another favorite task of Gabriel's comes as no surprise to those who know him, and it charms us all. Gabriel is the big brother figure to all youngsters who dwell in Heaven. Babies, toddlers, and children all receive Gabriel's attention and extra love. Not only does he play with them, but Gabriel reads to them, tells them stories, and teaches them about the wondrous home they now have. Few things warm my soul as does witnessing Gabriel with the young souls in Heaven.

Those youngsters are never sad, scared, or lonely. They remain content, safe, and loved. I see these precious young souls, and they are each beautiful, joyous, and full of laughter. Although their parents and loved ones grieve them, these young ones are free from any suffering or angst. I wish grieving parents could see their children in Heaven, so carefree, laughing, playing, learning, living eternally. If they could see their children just once, their immense grief would subside. Of course they will miss their beloved babies for the rest of their earthly lives, but they would no longer deeply mourn. They couldn't. Seeing Heaven's children fills me with joy and peace.

So does Archangel Michael, the leader of all angels and of God's army. As such, Michael is the one who combats Lucifer, or Satan as he is called as the ruler of Hell. Michael defeated Lucifer when Lucifer rebelled and rallied one-third of the angels to follow him. Lucifer and his fellow fallen angels were banished to Hell, where they remain.

Michael is a grand, gorgeous soldier of God, and he is a champion of all Christians. Michael escorts the newly deceased to their heavenly judgment. How he rejoices for every soul welcomed into Heaven! Michael's greatest desire is for everyone to live eternally in Heaven. But for those who do not, Michael weeps. He, too, knows the torments of Hell, and he does not wish that for anyone. Every time a soul is banished to Hell, Michael grieves. He cannot fathom why anyone would willingly forsake God and Heaven to spend eternity tortured in the fires of Hell. Neither can I.

Michael is the most beautiful angel I have ever seen. His beauty is an outward expression of the godliness, purity, and beauty of his being, his soul. Angels can never be what humans define as unattractive, for angels are filled with God and reflect His perfection.

Michael never backs away from a battle with Lucifer (Satan). Michael guarded Moses' tomb from Satan, as described in Jude 1:19: "Yet Michael, the archangel, when contending with the devil he disputed about the body of Moses, durst not bring against him a railing accusation, but said, The Lord rebuke thee." Michael will always defeat Satan, the former archangel Lucifer. Their final battle is foretold in Revelation 12:7-17.

Eventually, Satan will be put in the bottomless pit for 1,000 years, during which he shall not be allowed to tempt anyone (Revelation 20:1-3). At the end of the 1,000 years, Satan will be released from the pit, and he will resume his evil ways. He will gather the wicked to fight against God and His people. But God will bring down fire from Heaven to destroy the wicked. Satan will then be cast into the lake of fire to suffer eternal torment. Satan will never again tempt anyone; his reign of power will end (Revelation 20:7-10). This is reiterated in the Old Testament, in Nahum 1:9.

Lucifer knows his fate. He knows what awaits him. He understands the repercussions of his sin, yet he steadfastly refuses to let go of his pride and ask for God's forgiveness. How utterly sad this makes me. How could one who had been the preeminent angel in Heaven choose to spend eternity in Hell? Pride is a deadly sin for this very reason. "Pride goeth before destruction, and an haughty spirit before a fall," wrote Solomon in Proverbs 16:18.

Sin can never prosper nor profit on Earth. Humans are not perfect as were Adam and Eve prior to their fall. We each sin, some more than others. Many people do repent and ask for God's forgiveness. That is what He wants us to do. God does not want His children to forge a dysfunctional relationship with Him.

God is our Heavenly Father, and comparable to our earthly fathers. He loves us, wants the best for us, teaches us, and wishes us to obey Him. If we choose to disregard or to disobey Him, He will reprimand us—just as our earthly fathers should. When either of our fathers rebuke us, that is for our benefit. They do so because they do love us and wish the best for us, not because they do not care. If they truly did not care, they would do nothing and continue to let us commit wrong.

But neither of our fathers do that. They care too much. God does not want the separation between us to become permanent. He created us so that we would live with Him in Heaven for all time. Originally, the intention was that humans would live our earthly lives as stewards of the Earth, its animals, and its plants. We would work, sustain ourselves, love one another and God, and obey God.

Lucifer changed that by tempting Eve, who in turn tempted Adam. Both knowingly and willingly disobeyed God. That brought sin into the equation, and thus, through free will, opened the door for humans to choose sin.

Of course, God never wants us to choose sin, but He realizes that no human being attains perfection. He accepts that all humans sin. Even one of God's chosen—Moses—

sinned by not "sanctify[ing] God in the eyes of the people" (Numbers 20:12). Moses was punished for that sin, prohibited from entering the Promised Land of Israel. Moses' anger is an example of an all-too-common human response, but Numbers 20 proves how such reactions displease God.

John the Evangelist provides the antidote we need for sin. In 1 John 1:9, John tells us that "If we confess our sins he is faithful and just to forgive our sins and cleanse us from all unrighteousness." Simply put, to confess in this context means to agree with God; in other words, we need to see our sins as God sees them.

The Apostle Paul echoes this message in 2 Corinthians 7:10, telling us that "Godly sorrow brings repentance that leads to salvation and leaves no regret, but worldly sorrow brings death." What is worldly sorrow? This is the feeling some people have when they are caught doing wrong. They are not sorry for the wrong-doing, but rather for getting caught. There is no yearning to change their behavior, to stop the wrong-doing. There is only the wish to not get caught again.

Godly sorrow means we see our sins as Jesus sees us committing them. We see how our sins break His heart. We see our sins from Christ's perspective. The truth that my sins deeply wounded God my Father and Jesus my Savior did more than any other biblical lesson to lead me toward repentance. How could I deliberately hurt my Heavenly Father and my Savior? Why would I want to?

Not everyone feels this way, of course. While I lived on Earth, I heard many people claim that it was acceptable to sin, because they have impunity. How tragic and deluded. Grace does not mean people can sin without consequences. Far from that. In Ephesians 4:30, Apostle Paul clearly instructs us "And do not grieve the Holy Spirit of God, with whom you were sealed for the day of redemption." Do not aggrieve God, but rather seek to please Him, for you were branded as His own for the final deliverance from sin.

When I worked with the King Philippe High School chapter of Christ on Campus, one young man asked me a serious and thought-provoking question. "What if a Christian dies before he can repent of a sin? Would he still go to Heaven, or would he be condemned to Hell?" The students and I held a gloriously enlightening discussion and Bible study that afternoon. I began by assuring them that a Christian can die in sin and die without asking for forgiveness and go to Heaven—with one condition. That person must truly be saved. How can one know? We are saved by trusting Jesus Christ. Apostle Paul informs us so in Philippians 3:8-9.

Jesus paid for—He bought—our salvation with His blood, as Apostle Paul says in Romans 4:4-5: "Now to him that worketh is the reward not reckoned of grace, but of debt. But to him that worketh not, but believeth on him that justifieth the ungodly, his faith is counted for righteousness." Jesus Christ is our ticket to Heaven. All we need to do is trust Jesus Christ; trusting Him completely is the only way, not our actions or deeds. In order to gain an eternal home in Heaven, we must trust Jesus Christ.

What does it mean to trust Jesus? First, acknowledge that we cannot get ourselves into Heaven, not by our good deeds. We need to ask Jesus' forgiveness of our sins, and realize that He died for our sins. Afterward, a new life begins as a follower of Christ. As such, we rely upon Jesus for all aspects of our lives, not just for forgiveness of sin. Jesus becomes our primary teacher. We learn from Him. We learn how to live lives that are according to His will and His truth. We let Him guide us through our earthly lives. Doing so brings the utmost peace, joy, hope, and inner truth that one can ever experience. Trusting Jesus is truly life-changing.

Our true beliefs determine how we live. To trust Jesus expressly means that we believe, without question or doubt, what He tells us. If we do believe His statements are true, our lives will reflect that belief.

Those who say they trust Him, yet continue living the lives they crave, do not really trust Jesus. John the Evangelist and the Apostle Paul address this. John in 1 John 1:6-2:2, and Paul in Romans 6:1-2. "What shall we say then? Shall we continue in sin, that grace may abound? God forbid. How shall we, that are dead to sin, live any longer therein?" Why would we desire to become ensnared in sin once more? What is the gain in sin?

"But what about Adam and Eve? They sinned, and God punished them. Are they in Heaven?" another COC member asked. We examined the biblical evidence. After more than two hours of discussion, questions, and prayer for guidance, we had the answer. (Yes, I could have told them the answer, but I needed them to see the Truth.)

Yes, Adam and Eve disobeyed God and sinned against Him. However, they never lost their belief and trust in God. How do we know this? All the Bible reveals is that Eve gave birth to three sons after she and Adam were banished from Eden. By analyzing their son Abel, we get our answer.

Abel and his older brother Cain presented offerings to God. Abel's offering was by faith, as written in the New Testament Hebrews 11:4. To clarify, Cain's offering was not driven by his faith, but by his own yearning. Abel offered God the "more excellent sacrifice," the best he possessed. Cain did not give God his best. Abel offered with a heart that believed in God and through faith, whereas Cain kept his best for himself.

From where did Abel learn of God? From his parents, Adam and Eve, of course. Until Seth, the third son, was born, four humans existed on Earth: Adam, Eve, Cain, and Abel. Cain and Abel could never have learned about God elsewhere. Yes, Abel's faith was strong, while his brother's was weak, but both young men were taught the same. Remember, God infused Adam and Eve (and their descendants) with free will, and Cain chose what and how to believe.

Even after their expulsion from Eden, Adam and Eve knew God and taught their sons about Him. God never forsook them, either. In fact, God made clear, in the encounter with Adam, Eve, and the serpent, in the Garden of Eden, that Adam's and Eve's descendant would ultimately crush the serpent (Lucifer/Satan). As God told them, "I will put enmity between thy seed and her seed; it shall bruise thy head, and thou shalt bruise his heel" (Genesis 3:15).

Eve's seed would crush Satan. Who is this seed? Through Seth, in a genealogy containing the great prophets, Noah, Abraham, David, and Solomon, we get to Joseph, who wed Mary of Nazareth. Joseph was the man chosen by God to be the earthly father of the Savior, Jesus Christ (as provided in Matthew).

The genealogy to Mary of Nazareth is the same through David. However, David's son Nathan leads to Mary, and of course her son Jesus (traced in Luke).

Even though Adam and Eve sinned, they obviously asked God's forgiveness. They maintained their faith in God, which they taught to their two sons, even though Cain's faith was weak. Abel, however, proved his faith through his life and his actions. Because Adam and Eve believed and had faith, God made them the beginning of Jesus' earthly genealogy. God loves them. Therefore, Adam and Eve live in Heaven.

Another serious question a COC member asked me after a classmate's suicide is, "Can a Christian who commits suicide go to Heaven?" Of course suicide is wrong. Depression, the most common cause of suicide, is an understandably critical disorder that affects how one thinks, feels, and acts. Like with all disorders, the symptoms are not the choice of those who suffer. No one chooses this, and God understands that.

While I do comprehend how difficult depression, bullying, abuse, or any traumatic situation is, I want to remind everyone that a believer can always turn to God for peace and strength. God is stronger than any of us are, and He alone knows how everything will turn out at the end of the struggle. Even when we can't see the light and the hope, God can. He will always be there, through every trauma.

We all suffer during our earthly lives. God sometimes brings us to the point of utter despair and exasperation for a reason. He wants us to stop trying to live our earthly lives on our strength and will alone. He wants us instead to affix ourselves completely upon Christ.

Furthermore, only God knows when each of us will die. He knows the time of our deaths before we are even created. Job 14:5 clearly tells us this. "Seeing his days are determined, the number of his months are with thee, thou hast appointed his bounds that he cannot pass." Trust Jesus and follow Him. Allow God to determine how many days you will live.

That being said, the Bible never specifically says that suicide is an unforgiveable sin. Nothing can separate a true believer from God's love. The Apostle Paul reassures us of this twice in Romans 8, in 8:39 and in 8:1, when he writes,

"There is therefore now no condemnation to them which are in Christ Jesus, who walk not after the flesh, but after the Spirit."

Jonah, a true believer, got so angry that he longed to die. Job suffered horribly and wretchedly, and he, too, wanted to die. However, God stayed with Job while Satan tortured him, and He blessed Job after the suffering ended. No one will ever suffer as did Jesus on the cross. We would understand had He begged God to end His life, but He never did that. Instead, He knew his fate was God's will. He bore that unimaginable pain for us, never seeking to escape the pain and torture. He suffered for us, so that our sin can be forgiven.

God never wants anyone to commit suicide, but He also understands that the human body and mind can endure only so much pain and suffering. A true Christian is assured of getting to Heaven when he dies, even if by suicide.

This statement shocked the COC members, for they had been told that all murder is wrong, as stated in the sixth

Commandment. The first four Commandments direct us in our relationship with God. The remaining six Commandments instruct us in our relationships with other humans. None of them address how we treat ourselves. "Thou shalt not kill" (Exodus 20:13) refers to taking another person's life, not to suicide. Again, God does not condone suicide at all, but He never specifically states that it is an unforgiveable sin.

This discussion led to another important question: "Can any sin be forgiven?" The quick, short answer is no. Some people presume that the seven deadly sins cannot be forgiven, but that is false. These sins are discussed throughout scripture, although King Solomon does mention them in Proverbs 6:16-19: "These six things doth the Lord hate; yea, seven are an abomination unto him: A proud look, a lying tongue, and hands that shed innocent blood, An heart that deviseth wicked imaginations, feet that be swift in running to mischief, A false witness that speaketh lies, and he that soweth discord among brethren."

The seven deadly sins as we now identify them are lust (Matthew 5:28), gluttony (Proverbs 23:21), greed (Ephesians 4:19), sloth (Proverbs 115:19), wrath (Proverbs 15:1), envy (1 Peter 2:1-2), and pride (Proverbs 16:18). Although these sins are completely forgivable by God, this does not mean people should commit them. All sin displeases God.

However, He will forgive all but one sin if we repent and ask His forgiveness. In three separate Bible verses, Jesus Himself tells us which sin remains unforgiveable. Mark 3:28-29 and Luke 12:8-10 are two. In Matthew 12:31-32, Jesus declares, "Wherefore I say to you, All manner of sin and blasphemy shall be forgiven unto men: but the blasphemy against the Holy Ghost shall not be forgiven unto men. And whosoever speaketh a word against the Son of man, it shall be forgiven him: but whosoever speaketh against the Holy Ghost, it shall not be forgiven him, neither in this world, nor in the world to come."

What does it mean to blaspheme the Holy Ghost? There is but one way: deny the Holy Ghost's witness to Jesus. Reject Christ.

Mark 3:29 calls it the eternal sin. Rejecting—denying—Jesus is the only unforgivable sin. As Stephen said in his sermon, recorded by Luke in Acts 7:51, "Ye stiffnecked and uncircumcised in heart and ears, ye do always resist the Holy Ghost: as your fathers did, so do ye." Stephen convicted the congregation's Jewish leaders of killing Jesus Christ, just as their ancestors had persecuted God's prophets. The Jews to whom Stephen spoke had rejected the Savior whom the prophets had foretold. These Jews who demanded that the Romans crucify Jesus were descendants of Abraham, but they never truly believed that they would receive God's blessings only if they accepted Jesus Christ as their Savior. They denied Him. They committed the one unforgivable sin.

Most Christians who fear they have blasphemed the Holy Ghost live with the unwarranted angst of believing they aren't going to Heaven. Unwarranted? How? This is a very severe issue. Of course it is. However, most Christians do not deny Jesus as the Lord and Savior. Most do not give Lucifer credit for the Holy Ghost's work or praise Lucifer for their blessings. True Christians who do ask for God's forgiveness of their sins and claim Jesus Christ as their Savior will enter the gates of Heaven.

"What do the gates of Heaven look like?" Most depictions I saw when I lived on Earth showed gleaming, ornate golden gates that open wide when a soul is accepted into Heaven. These gates always reminded me of those I often saw at mansions, palaces, or even cemeteries. This is not what Heaven's gates look like, though.

The Apostle Paul tells us exactly what the gates of Heaven look like in Revelation, the book that came to him from Jesus via Gabriel. In Chapter 21, Verse 21, John writes, "And the twelve gates were twelve pearls: every several gate was of one pearl: and the street of the city was pure gold, as it were transparent glass." How glorious! Heaven contains all of God's Creations: gems, precious metals, trees, plants, and animals.

Yes, animals live in Heaven when their earthly lives end. After all, animals are the second most important inhabitants of Earth. God entrusts animals to our care and conservation. Furthermore, our relationships with animals form meaningful aspects of our lives.

Both the Old Testament and the New Testament assure us that animals dwell in Heaven. Isaiah 65:25 tells us that "The wolf and the lamb shall feed together, and the lion shall eat straw like the bullock: and dust shall be the serpent's meat. They shall not hurt or destroy in all my holy mountain, saith the Lord." The holy mountain is Heaven. This verse also proves that animals will no longer hunt and kill prey for food; their every need, like ours, is provided. There will never be any murder in Heaven for any reason, not even for food.

Job 12:10 reiterates this by telling us that, "In whose hand is the soul of every living thing, and the breath of all mankind." Every living being, human and animal, has a spirit, the breath of God.

The Apostle Paul, relaying Jesus' words, confirms that "every creature which is in Heaven, and on earth, and under the earth, and such as are in the sea, and all that are in them, heard I saying, Blessing, and honour, and glory, and power, be unto him that sitteth upon the throne, and unto the Lamb for ever and ever" (Revelation 5:13). Every creature will praise God in Heaven.

If my testimony counts, I, too, can comfort you that animals reside in Heaven. I have seen thousands, and even frequently witness lions, bears, and wolves sitting or walking alongside deer, zebras, and rabbits. Matthew often paints them. On a personal note, my beloved Palomino, Starlight, is here, as is my father's handsome stallion Midnight. We often ride them across the lush, green fields of Heaven.

Heaven truly is more glorious than any words could ever convey.

Often in conversations with elderly, ill, or incapacitated people, I was asked why God kept them alive. They remained limited in what they could do, and they wanted to go to Heaven. God is quite aware of this desire, for the Apostle Paul writes in Philippians 1:23, "For I am betwixt two, having a desire to depart, and to be with Christ; which is better."

Do not feel guilty for asking God to take you to Heaven. Do realize, though, that He has reasons for keeping you on Earth. Ask Him to show you what His reasons are. "They shall bring forth fruit in old age; they shall be fat and flourishing" says Psalm 92:14. Age produces wisdom, experience, and maturity which can be productive.

Ask God to help you to be a witness for Him. Your life can become a powerful testimony, especially if you accept that God has a reason for keeping you on Earth. If you can show God's love and peace even in your situation, you will stand tall as a witness for God. You can help to bring others closer to God. As Paul wrote to Timothy, "For therefore we both labour and suffer reproach, because we trust in the living God, who is the Saviour of all men, specially of those that believe" (1 Timothy 4:10). Yes, I know how difficult it can be to maintain hope and peace when you hurt or suffer or feel despondent. I do.

Remember, though, that you are loved and valuable. You have a purpose, no matter how dire your circumstances may seem. Trust that God will remain with you and will use you to glorify Him. I once met an elderly woman named Maggie who lost her speech to a stroke that also debilitated her right side. Even though she could not speak, she continuously let people know how much God had done for her. Many people were shocked by that. Didn't God cause her stroke, after all? People asked her that. Her answer, written in shaky print with her non-dominant hand, was, "No. I caused my stroke. I made poor choices in my life that led me here. My fault. Not God's. But I am alive. I can watch my great-grandchildren grow. I can smell flowers. I can read my Bible. I can live for God. He has blessed me, even though I made many mistakes. When I do die, I will kiss His feet and thank Him." What a beautiful testimony!

This woman's story leads to a question I was often asked on Earth: "Will I see God?" No matter what else you do on Earth, the point is to put God first, to put Him into your heart and into your mind, and to let Him guide you. Live, respond to others, and work as a child of God. Let God shine forth in everything you do.

Will you see God when you enter Heaven? Yes! Jesus promises believers that we will see God face-to-face. In His Sermon on the Mount, Jesus proclaims eight blessings. "Blessed are the pure in heart: for they shall see God" (Matthew 5:8) is the sixth blessing He mentions.

We shall remain in continuous, unbroken fellowship and oneness with God, without the separation we have on Earth. Sin currently separates people from face-to-face contact with God. Once we enter those pearly gates of Heaven, we become sinless. Jesus, through the Apostle John, also assures us this in Revelation 21:3. "And I heard a great voice out of heaven saying, Behold, the tabernacle of God is with men, and he will dwell with them, and they shall be his people, and God himself shall be with them, and be their God." Amazing to ponder, right?

I have seen God. I have talked with Him. Nothing compares to seeing, to meeting, my Heavenly Father. I would never exist without Him, nor would I want to exist without God. My prayer is that you feel likewise, and that you will submit to Him. Open your heart, let God dwell there, claim Jesus as your Savior, and you will earn an eternal home in Heaven.

Why would you want to spend eternity elsewhere? Where else could you experience the deepest, truest love?

Love. Love is the heart of all of Creation. We were created from God's love. We are the manifestations of His love. The Earth upon which we live our physical lives was created from that same love, as a place that provides all we need in order to live those lives. Its beauty and wonder are manifestations of His love. Look around, and you will see His love in the sunrise, in a snowflake, in a soaring bird, in a majestic mountain, in a growing flower. Everything was created from that most perfect love.

So, too, was Heaven. God created Heaven as our eternal home. When we have finished our lives on Earth, and if we have reciprocated God's love for us, we will live in Heaven forevermore. Heaven is difficult to describe, for mere words can never capture the awesome wonder, beauty, and peace of Heaven. Heaven is the only place to ever exist where there is no strife, no pain, no sickness, no night, no hunger, no death, and no hatred. Love is all that exists in Heaven. Love fills Heaven and all who dwell here.

God's love for us fills Heaven and us. That love is so powerful and immense that there is no room for any other feeling. That love is the most comforting we will ever know. Heaven contains the most glorious beauty, beauty beyond human comprehension or imagination. True perfection exists only in Heaven, for Heaven is the only place untainted by the evils and ills that plague Earth.

You will never feel pain, sorrow, exhaustion, hunger, heartbreak, regret, anger, resentment. You will feel only peace, joy, and love. You will become a new creature made entirely of love. All of the baggage of your earthly life will leave you when you die and enter the gates of Heaven and begin your eternal life. You will still be you, but you will be reborn whole and perfect. Your physical life will end. Your spiritual life will never end. That is your reward for loving God as He loves you. No greater love exists than God's love for each of us, and Heaven is the proof of that love.

Author's Information

Sheilah R. Craft is an English professor, writer, blogger, poet, artist, ardent genealogist, and book lover. Born and raised in the Midwestern United States, Sheilah was born surrounded by a close family—including several educators—books, and animals. She began reading and writing very early, and has published novels, short stories, articles, and poems. She was literally born a writer. Her series of novels centered on the lives of one family dynasty and spanning more than two centuries began in the fall of 2012 with the first volume, Heart-Glow. The second volume, First Love Never Dies, was published in the spring of 2013. Heart Eternal, the third volume in the series, was published in the spring of 2014, while Life Eternal, the fourth volume, was published in 2015. The Splendor of Heaven is the fifth volume. One more volume is planned which will conclude the Heart-Glow series.

BOOKS BY SHEILAH R CRAFT

Published by <u>STARLIGHT Books:</u>

•HEART-GLOW: A NOVEL

•FIRST LOVE NEVER DIES: HEART-GLOW
VOLUME II

•HEART ETERNAL: HEART-GLOW VOLUME III

•LIFE ETERNAL: HEART-GLOW VOLUME IV

•THE SPLENDOR OF HEAVEN: HEART-GLOW
VOLUME V

•MARY MAGDALENE: A MYSTERY PLAY

Published by <u>Little Butterfly:</u>

•THE QUEST FOR PERFECTION: SHELLEY AND
THE POET-HERO

•A DAY WITH TEDDY BEAR

www.ingramcontent.com/pod-product-compliance
Lightning Source LLC
Chambersburg PA
CBHW081919130726
47909CB00015B/3033